The Red Pony

by John Steinbeck

BANTAM BOOKS

TORONTO • NEW YORK • LONDON • SYDNEY • AUCKLAND

This low-priced Bantam Book
has been completely reset in a type face
designed for easy reading, and was printed
from new plates. It contains the complete
text of the original hard-cover edition.
NOT ONE WORD HAS BEEN OMITTED.

RL 4, IL age 10 and up

THE RED PONY

A Bantam Book / published by arrangement with
The Viking Press, Inc.

PRINTING HISTORY

Originally published by Covici-Friede September 1937
Viking edition published September 1945
2nd printing . . . October 1945
Book-of-the-Month Club edition published September 1945
Bantam edition / August 1948
New Bantam edition / December 1955
70 printings through November 1983

Bantam Books are published by Bantam Books, Inc. Its trademark, consisting of the words "Bantam Books" and the portrayal of a rooster, is Registered in U.S. Patent and Trademark Office and in other countries. Marca Registrada. Bantam Books, Inc., 666 Fifth Avenue, New York, New York 10103.

PRINTED IN THE UNITED STATES OF AMERICA

H   79

THE RED PONY

THE RED PONY

THE RED PONY

I. THE GIFT

AT DAYBREAK Billy Buck emerged from the bunkhouse and stood for a moment on the porch looking up at the sky. He was a broad, bandy-legged little man with a walrus mustache, with square hands, puffed and muscled on the palms. His eyes were a contemplative, watery grey and the hair which protruded from under his Stetson hat was spiky and weathered. Billy was still stuffing his shirt into his blue jeans as he stood on the porch. He unbuckled his belt and tightened it again. The belt showed, by the worn shiny places opposite each hole, the gradual increase of Billy's middle over a period of years. When he had seen to the weather, Billy cleared each nostril by holding its mate closed with his forefinger and blowing fiercely. Then he walked down to the barn, rubbing his hands together. He curried and brushed two saddle horses in the stalls, talking quietly to them all the time; and he had hardly finished when the iron triangle started ringing at the ranch house. Billy stuck the brush and currycomb together and laid them on the rail, and went up to breakfast. His action had been so deliberate and yet so wasteless of time that he came to the house while Mrs. Tiflin was still ringing the triangle. She nodded her grey head to him and withdrew into the kitchen. Billy Buck sat down on the steps, because he was a cow-hand, and it wouldn't be fitting that he should go first into the dining-room. He heard Mr. Tiflin in the house, stamping his feet into his boots.

The high jangling note of the triangle put the boy Jody in motion. He was only a little boy, ten years old, with hair like dusty yellow grass and with shy polite grey eyes, and with a mouth that worked when he thought. The triangle picked him up out of sleep. It didn't occur to him to disobey the harsh note. He never had: no one he knew ever had. He brushed the tangled hair out of his eyes and skinned his nightgown off. In a moment he was dressed—blue chambray shirt and overalls. It was late in the summer, so of course there were no shoes to bother with. In the kitchen he waited until his mother got from in front of the sink and went back to the stove. Then he washed himself and brushed back his wet hair with his fingers. His mother turned sharply on him as he left the sink. Jody looked shyly away.

"I've got to cut your hair before long," his mother said. "Breakfast's on the table. Go on in, so Billy can come."

Jody sat at the long table which was covered with white oilcloth washed through to the fabric in some places. The fried eggs lay in rows on their platter. Jody took three eggs on his plate and followed with three thick slices of crisp bacon. He carefully scraped a spot of blood from one of the egg yolks.

Billy Buck clumped in. "That won't hurt you," Billy explained. "That's only a sign the rooster leaves."

Jody's tall stern father came in then and Jody knew from the noise on the floor that he was wearing boots, but he looked under the table anyway, to make sure. His father turned off the oil lamp over the table, for plenty of morning light now came through the windows.

Jody did not ask where his father and Billy Buck were riding that day, but he wished he might go along. His father was a disciplinarian. Jody obeyed him in everything without questions of any kind. Now, Carl Tiflin sat down and reached for the egg platter.

"Got the cows ready to go, Billy?" he asked.

"In the lower corral," Billy said. "I could just as well take them in alone."

"Sure you could. But a man needs company. Besides your throat gets pretty dry." Carl Tiflin was jovial this morning.

Jody's mother put her head in the door. "What time do you think to be back, Carl?"

"I can't tell. I've got to see some men in Salinas. Might be gone till dark."

The eggs and coffee and big biscuits disappeared rapidly. Jody followed the two men out of the house. He watched them mount their horses and drive six old milk cows out of the corral and start over the hill toward Salinas. They were going to sell the old cows to the butcher.

When they had disappeared over the crown of the ridge Jody walked up the hill in back of the house. The dogs trotted around the house corner hunching their shoulders and grinning horribly with pleasure. Jody patted their heads—Doubletree Mutt with the big thick tail and yellow eyes, and Smasher, the shepherd, who had killed a coyote and lost an ear in doing it. Smasher's one good ear stood up higher than a collie's ear should. Billy Buck said that always happened. After the frenzied greeting the dogs lowered their noses to the ground in a businesslike way and went ahead, looking back now and then to make sure that the boy was coming. They walked up through the chicken yard and saw the quail eating with the chickens. Smasher chased the chickens a little to keep in practice in case there should ever be sheep to herd. Jody continued on through the large vegetable patch where the green corn was higher than his head.

The cow-pumpkins were green and small yet. He went on to the sagebrush line where the cold spring ran out of its pipe and fell into a round wooden tub. He leaned over and drank close to the green mossy wood where the water tasted best. Then he turned and looked back on the ranch, on the low, whitewashed house girded with red geraniums, and on the long bunkhouse by the cypress tree where Billy Buck lived alone. Jody could see the great black kettle under the cypress tree. That was where the pigs were scalded. The sun was coming over the ridge now, glaring on the whitewash of the houses and barns, making the wet grass blaze softly. Behind him, in the tall sagebrush, the birds were scampering on the ground, making a great noise among the dry leaves; the squirrels piped shrilly on the side-hills. Jody looked along at the farm buildings. He felt an uncertainty in the air, a feeling of change and of loss and of the gain of new and unfamiliar things. Over the hillside two big black buzzards sailed low to the ground and their shadows slipped smoothly and quickly ahead of them. Some animal had died in the vicinity. Jody knew it. It might be a cow or it might be the remains of a rabbit. The buzzards overlooked nothing. Jody hated them as all decent things hate them, but they could not be hurt because they made away with carrion.

After a while the boy sauntered down hill again. The dogs had long ago given him up and gone into the brush to do things in their own way. Back through the vegetable garden he went, and he paused for a moment to smash a green muskmelon with his heel, but he was not happy about it. It was a bad thing to do, he knew perfectly well. He kicked dirt over the ruined melon to conceal it.

Back at the house his mother bent over his rough hands, inspecting his fingers and nails. It did little good to start him clean to school for too many things could happen on the way. She sighed over the black cracks on his fingers, and then gave him his books and his lunch and started him on the mile walk to school. She noticed that his mouth was working a good deal this morning.

Jody started his journey. He filled his pockets with little pieces of white quartz that lay in the road, and every so often he took a shot at a bird or at some rabbit that had stayed sunning itself in the road too long. At the crossroads over the bridge he met two friends and the three of them walked to school together, making ridiculous strides and being rather silly. School had just opened two weeks before. There was still a spirit of revolt among the pupils.

It was four o'clock in the afternoon when Jody topped the hill and looked down on the ranch again. He looked for the saddle horses, but the corral was empty. His father was not back yet. He went slowly, then, toward the afternoon chores. At the ranch house, he found his mother sitting on the porch, mending socks.

"There's two doughnuts in the kitchen for you," she said. Jody slid to the kitchen, and returned with half of one of the doughnuts already eaten and his mouth full. His mother asked him what he had learned in school that day, but she didn't listen to his doughnut-muffled answer. She interrupted, "Jody, tonight see you fill the wood-box clear full. Last night you crossed the sticks and it wasn't only about half full. Lay the sticks flat tonight. And Jody, some of the hens are hiding eggs, or else the dogs are eating them. Look about in the grass and see if you can find any nests."

Jody, still eating, went out and did his chores. He saw the quail come down to eat with the chickens when he threw out the grain. For some reason his father was proud to have them come. He never allowed any shooting near the house for fear the quail might go away.

7

When the wood-box was full, Jody took his twenty-two rifle up to the cold spring at the brush line. He drank again and then aimed the gun at all manner of things, at rocks, at birds on the wing, at the big black pig kettle under the cypress tree, but he didn't shoot for he had no cartridges and wouldn't have until he was twelve. If his father had seen him aim the rifle in the direction of the house he would have put the cartridges off another year. Jody remembered this and did not point the rifle down the hill again. Two years was enough to wait for cartridges. Nearly all of his father's presents were given with reservations which hampered their value somewhat. It was good discipline.

The supper waited until dark for his father to return. When at last he came in with Billy Buck, Jody could smell the delicious brandy on their breaths. Inwardly he rejoiced, for his father sometimes talked to him when he smelled of brandy, sometimes even told things he had done in the wild days when he was a boy.

After supper, Jody sat by the fireplace and his shy polite eyes sought the room corners, and he waited for his father to tell what it was he contained, for Jody knew he had news of some sort. But he was disappointed. His father pointed a stern finger at him.

"You'd better go to bed, Jody. I'm going to need you in the morning."

That wasn't so bad. Jody liked to do the things he had to do as long as they weren't routine things. He looked at the floor and his mouth worked out a question before he spoke it. "What are we going to do in the morning, kill a pig?" he asked softly.

"Never you mind. You better get to bed."

When the door was closed behind him, Jody heard his father and Billy Buck chuckling and he knew it was a joke of some kind. And later, when he lay in bed, trying to make words out of murmurs in the other room, he heard his father protest, "But, Ruth, I didn't give much for him."

Jody heard the hoot-owls hunting mice down by the barn, and he heard a fruit tree limb tap-tapping against the house. A cow was lowing when he went to sleep.

When the triangle sounded in the morning, Jody dressed more quickly even than usual. In the kitchen, while he washed his face and combed back his hair, his mother addressed him irritably. "Don't you go out until you get a good breakfast in you."

He went into the dining-room and sat at the long white table. He took a steaming hotcake from the platter, arranged two fried eggs on it, covered them with another hotcake and squashed the whole thing with his fork.

His father and Billy Buck came in. Jody knew from the sound of the floor that both of them were wearing flatheeled shoes, but he peered under the table to make sure. His father turned off the oil lamp, for the day had arrived, and he looked stern and disciplinary, but Billy Buck didn't look at Jody at all. He avoided the shy questioning eyes of the boy and soaked a whole piece of toast in his coffee.

Carl Tiflin said crossly, "You come with us after breakfast!"

Jody had trouble with his food then, for he felt a kind of doom in the air. After Billy had tilted his saucer and drained the coffee which had slopped into it, and had wiped his hands on his jeans, the two men stood up from the table and went out into the morning light together, and Jody respectfully followed a little behind them. He tried to keep his mind from running ahead, tried to keep it absolutely motionless.

His mother called, "Carl! Don't you let it keep him from school."

They marched past the cypress, where a singletree hung from a limb to butcher the pigs on, and past the black iron kettle, so it was not a pig killing. The sun shone over the hill and threw long, dark shadows of the trees and buildings. They crossed a stubble-field to short-cut to the barn. Jody's father unhooked the door and they went in. They had been walking toward the sun on the way down. The barn was black as night in contrast and warm from the hay and from the beasts. Jody's father moved over toward the one box stall. "Come here!" he ordered. Jody could begin to see things now. He looked into the box stall and then stepped back quickly.

A red pony colt was looking at him out of the stall. Its tense ears were forward and a light of disobedience was in its eyes. Its coat was rough and thick as an airedale's fur and its mane was long and tangled. Jody's throat collapsed in on itself and cut his breath short.

"He needs a good currying," his father said, "and if I ever hear of you not feeding him or leaving his stall dirty, I'll sell him off in a minute."

Jody couldn't bear to look at the pony's eyes any more. He gazed down at his hands for a moment, and he asked very shyly, "Mine?" No one answered him. He put his hand out toward the pony. Its grey nose came close, sniffing loudly, and then the lips drew back and the strong teeth closed on Jody's fingers. The pony shook its head up and down and seemed to laugh with amusement. Jody regarded his bruised fingers. "Well," he said with pride— "Well, I guess he can bite all right." The two men laughed, somewhat in relief. Carl Tiflin went out of the barn and walked up a side-hill to be by himself, for he was embarrassed, but Billy Buck stayed. It was easier to talk to Billy Buck. Jody asked again—"Mine?"

Billy became professional in tone. "Sure! That is, if

you look out for him and break him right. I'll show you how. He's just a colt. You can't ride him for some time."

Jody put out his bruised hand again, and this time the red pony let his nose be rubbed. "I ought to have a carrot," Jody said. "Where'd we get him, Billy?"

"Bought him at a sheriff's auction," Billy explained. "A show went broke in Salinas and had debts. The sheriff was selling off their stuff."

The pony stretched out his nose and shook the forelock from his wild eyes. Jody stroked the nose a little. He said softly, "There isn't a—saddle?"

Billy Buck laughed. "I'd forgot. Come along."

In the harness room he lifted down a little saddle of red morocco leather. "It's just a show saddle," Billy Buck said disparagingly. "It isn't practical for the brush, but it was cheap at the sale."

Jody couldn't trust himself to look at the saddle either, and he couldn't speak at all. He brushed the shining red leather with his fingertips, and after a long time he said, "It'll look pretty on him though." He thought of the grandest and prettiest things he knew. "If he hasn't a name already, I think I'll call him Gabilan Mountains," he said.

Billy Buck knew how he felt. "It's a pretty long name. Why don't you just call him Gabilan? That means hawk. That would be a fine name for him." Billy felt glad. "If you will collect tail hair, I might be able to make a hair rope for you sometime. You could use it for a hackamore."

Jody wanted to go back to the box stall. "Could I lead him to school, do you think—to show the kids?"

But Billy shook his head. "He's not even halter-broke yet. We had a time getting him here. Had to almost drag him. You better be starting for school though."

"I'll bring the kids to see him here this afternoon," Jody said.

Six boys came over the hill half an hour early that afternoon, running hard, their heads down, their fore-arms working, their breath whistling. They swept by the house and cut across the stubble-field to the barn. And then they stood self-consciously before the pony, and then they looked at Jody with eyes in which there was a new admiration and a new respect. Before today Jody had been a boy, dressed in overalls and a blue shirt—quieter than most, even suspected of being a little cow-ardly. And now he was different. Out of a thousand centuries they drew the ancient admiration of the foot-man for the horseman. They knew instinctively that a man on a horse is spiritually as well as physically bigger than a man on foot. They knew that Jody had been mi-raculously lifted out of equality with them, and had been placed over them. Gabilan put his head out of the stall and sniffed them.

"Why'nt you ride him?" the boys cried. "Why'nt you braid his tail with ribbons like in the fair?" "When you going to ride him?"

Jody's courage was up. He too felt the superiority of the horseman. "He's not old enough. Nobody can ride him for a long time. I'm going to train him on the long halter. Billy Buck is going to show me how."

"Well, can't we even lead him around a little?"

"He isn't even halter broke," Jody said. He wanted to be completely alone when he took the pony out the first time. "Come and see the saddle."

They were speechless at the red morocco saddle, com-pletely shocked out of comment. "It isn't much use in the brush," Jody explained. "It'll look pretty on him though. Maybe I'll ride bareback when I go into the brush."

"How you going to rope a cow without a saddle horn?"

"Maybe I'll get another saddle for every day. My father might want me to help him with the stock." He let them feel the red saddle, and showed them the brass chain throat-latch on the bridle and the big brass buttons at each temple where the headstall and brow band crossed. The whole thing was too wonderful. They had to go away after a little while, and each boy, in his mind, searched among his possessions for a bribe worthy of offering in return for a ride on the red pony when the time should come.

Jody was glad when they had gone. He took brush and currycomb from the wall, took down the barrier of the box stall and stepped cautiously in. The pony's eyes glittered, and he edged around into kicking position. But Jody touched him on the shoulder and rubbed his high arched neck as he had always seen Billy Buck do, and he crooned, "So-o-o Boy," in a deep voice. The pony gradually relaxed his tenseness. Jody curried and brushed until a pile of dead hair lay in the stall and until the pony's coat had taken on a deep red shine. Each time he finished he thought it might have been done better. He braided the mane into a dozen little pigtails, and he braided the forelock, and then he undid them and brushed the hair out straight again.

Jody did not hear his mother enter the barn. She was angry when she came, but when she looked in at the pony and at Jody working over him, she felt a curious pride rise up in her. "Have you forgot the wood-box?" she asked gently. "It's not far off from dark and there's not a stick of wood in the house, and the chickens aren't fed."

Jody quickly put up his tools. "I forgot, ma'am."

"Well, after this do your chores first. Then you won't forget. I expect you'll forget lots of things now if I don't keep an eye on you."

"Can I have carrots from the garden for him, ma'am?"

She had to think about that. "Oh—I guess so, if you only take the big tough ones."

"Carrots keep the coat good," he said, and again she felt the curious rush of pride.

Jody never waited for the triangle to get him out of bed after the coming of the pony. It became his habit to creep out of bed even before his mother was awake, to slip into his clothes and to go quietly down to the barn to see Gabilan. In the grey quiet mornings when the land and the brush and the houses and the trees were silver-grey and black like a photograph negative, he stole toward the barn, past the sleeping stones and the sleeping cypress tree. The turkeys, roosting in the tree out of coyotes' reach, clicked drowsily. The fields glowed with a grey frost-like light and in the dew the tracks of rabbits and of field mice stood out sharply. The good dogs came stiffly out of their little houses, hackles up and deep growls in their throats. Then they caught Jody's scent, and their stiff tails rose up and waved a greeting— Doubletree Mutt with the big thick tail, and Smasher, the incipient shepherd—then went lazily back to their warm beds.

It was a strange time and a mysterious journey, to Jody —an extension of a dream. When he first had the pony he liked to torture himself during the trip by thinking Gabilan would not be in his stall, and worse, would never have been there. And he had other delicious little self-induced pains. He thought how the rats had gnawed ragged holes in the red saddle, and how the mice had nibbled Gabilan's tail until it was stringy and thin. He usually ran the last little way to the barn. He unlatched the rusty hasp of the barn door and stepped in, and no matter how quietly he opened the door, Gabilan was always looking at him over the barrier of the box stall and Gabilan whinnied softly and stamped his front foot, and his eyes had big sparks of red fire in them like oak-wood embers.

Sometimes, if the work horses were to be used that day, Jody found Billy Buck in the barn harnessing and currying. Billy stood with him and looked long at Gabilan and he told Jody a great many things about horses. He explained that they were terribly afraid for their feet, so that one must make a practice of lifting the legs and patting the hoofs and ankles to remove their terror. He told Jody how horses love conversation. He must talk to the pony all the time, and tell him the reasons for everything. Billy wasn't sure a horse could understand everything that was said to him, but it was impossible to say how much was understood. A horse never kicked up a fuss if some one he liked explained things to him. Billy could give examples, too. He had known, for instance, a horse nearly dead beat with fatigue to perk up when told it was only a little farther to his destination. And he had known a horse paralyzed with fright to come out of it when his rider told him what it was that was frightening him. While he talked in the mornings, Billy Buck cut twenty or thirty straws into neat three-inch lengths and stuck them into his hatband. Then during the whole day, if he wanted to pick his teeth or merely to chew on something, he had only to reach up for one of them.

Jody listened carefully, for he knew and the whole country knew that Billy Buck was a fine hand with horses. Billy's own horse was a stringy cayuse with a hammer head, but he nearly always won the first prizes at the stock trials. Billy could rope a steer, take a double half-hitch about the horn with his riata, and dismount, and his horse would play the steer as an angler plays a fish, keeping a tight rope until the steer was down or beaten.

Every morning, after Jody had curried and brushed the pony, he let down the barrier of the stall, and Gabilan thrust past him and raced down the barn and into the corral. Around and around he galloped, and sometimes he jumped forward and landed on stiff legs. He stood quivering, stiff ears forward, eyes rolling so that the whites showed, pretending to be frightened. At last he walked snorting to the water-trough and buried his nose in the water up to the nostrils. Jody was proud then, for he knew that was the way to judge a horse. Poor horses only touched their lips to the water, but a fine spirited beast put his whole nose and mouth under, and only left room to breathe.

Then Jody stood and watched the pony, and he saw things he had never noticed about any other horse, the sleek, sliding flank muscles and the cords of the buttocks, which flexed like a closing fist, and the shine the sun put on the red coat. Having seen horses all his life, Jody had never looked at them very closely before. But now he noticed the moving ears which gave expression and even inflection of expression to the face. The pony talked with his ears. You could tell exactly how he felt about everything by the way his ears pointed. Sometimes they were stiff and upright and sometimes lax and sagging. They went back when he was angry or fearful, and forward when he was anxious and curious and pleased; and their exact position indicated which emotion he had.

Billy Buck kept his word. In the early fall the training began. First there was the halter-breaking, and that was the hardest because it was the first thing. Jody held a carrot and coaxed and promised and pulled on the rope.

The pony set his feet like a burro when he felt the strain. But before long he learned. Jody walked all over the ranch leading him. Gradually he took to dropping the rope until the pony followed him unled wherever he went.

And then came the training on the long halter. That was slower work. Jody stood in the middle of a circle, holding the long halter. He clucked with his tongue and the pony started to walk in a big circle, held in by the long rope. He clucked again to make the pony trot, and again to make him gallop. Around and around Gabilan went thundering and enjoying it immensely. Then he called, "Whoa," and the pony stopped. It was not long until Gabilan was perfect at it. But in many ways he was a bad pony. He bit Jody in the pants and stomped on Jody's feet. Now and then his ears went back and he aimed a tremendous kick at the boy. Every time he did one of these bad things, Gabilan settled back and seemed to laugh to himself.

Billy Buck worked at the hair rope in the evenings before the fireplace. Jody collected tail hair in a bag, and he sat and watched Billy slowly constructing the rope, twisting a few hairs to make a string and rolling two strings together for a cord, and then braiding a number of cords to make the rope. Billy rolled the finished rope on the floor under his foot to make it round and hard.

The long halter work rapidly approached perfection. Jody's father, watching the pony stop and start and trot and gallop, was a little bothered by it.

"He's getting to be almost a trick pony," he complained. "I don't like trick horses. It takes all the—dignity out of a horse to make him do tricks. Why, a trick horse is kind of like an actor—no dignity, no character of his own." And his father said, "I guess you better be getting him used to the saddle pretty soon."

Jody rushed for the harness-room. For some time he had been riding the saddle on a sawhorse. He changed the stirrup length over and over, and could never get it just right. Sometimes, mounted on the sawhorse in the harness-room, with collars and hames and tugs hung all about him, Jody rode out beyond the room. He carried his rifle across the pommel. He saw the fields go flying by, and he heard the beat of the galloping hoofs.

It was a ticklish job, saddling the pony the first time. Gabilan hunched and reared and threw the saddle off before the cinch could be tightened. It had to be replaced again and again until at last the pony let it stay. And the cinching was difficult, too. Day by day Jody tightened the girth a little more until at last the pony didn't mind the saddle at all.

Then there was the bridle. Billy explained how to use a stick of licorice for a bit until Gabilan was used to having something in his mouth. Billy explained, "Of course we could force-break him to everything, but he wouldn't be as good a horse if we did. He'd always be a little bit afraid, and he wouldn't mind because he wanted to."

The first time the pony wore the bridle he whipped his head about and worked his tongue against the bit until the blood oozed from the corners of his mouth. He tried to rub the headstall off on the manger. His ears pivoted about and his eyes turned red with fear and with general rambunctiousness. Jody rejoiced, for he knew that only a mean-souled horse does not resent training.

And Jody trembled when he thought of the time when he would first sit in the saddle. The pony would probably throw him off. There was no disgrace in that. The disgrace would come if he did not get right up and mount again. Sometimes he dreamed that he lay in the dirt and cried and couldn't make himself mount again. The shame of the dream lasted until the middle of the day.

Gabilan was growing fast. Already he had lost the long-leggedness of the colt; his mane was getting longer and blacker. Under the constant currying and brushing his coat lay as smooth and gleaming as orange-red lacquer. Jody oiled the hoofs and kept them carefully trimmed so they would not crack.

The hair rope was nearly finished. Jody's father gave him an old pair of spurs and bent in the side bars and cut down the strap and took up the chainlets until they fitted. And then one day Carl Tiflin said:

"The pony's growing faster than I thought. I guess you can ride him by Thanksgiving. Think you can stick on?"

"I don't know," Jody said shyly. Thanksgiving was only three weeks off. He hoped it wouldn't rain, for rain would spot the red saddle.

Gabilan knew and liked Jody by now. He nickered when Jody came across the stubble-field, and in the pasture he came running when his master whistled for him. There was always a carrot for him every time.

Billy Buck gave him riding instructions over and over. "Now when you get up there, just grab tight with your knees and keep your hands away from the saddle, and if you get throwed, don't let that stop you. No matter how good a man is, there's always some horse can pitch him. You just climb up again before he gets to feeling smart about it. Pretty soon, he won't throw you no more, and pretty soon he *can't* throw you no more. That's the way to do it."

"I hope it don't rain before," Jody said.

"Why not? Don't want to get throwed in the mud?"

That was partly it, and also he was afraid that in the flurry of bucking Gabilan might slip and fall on him and break his leg or his hip. He had seen that happen to men before, had seen how they writhed on the ground like squashed bugs, and he was afraid of it.

He practiced on the sawhorse how he would hold the reins in his left hand and a hat in his right hand. If he kept his hands thus busy, he couldn't grab the horn if he felt himself going off. He didn't like to think of what would happen if he did grab the horn. Perhaps his father and Billy Buck would never speak to him again, they would be so ashamed. The news would get about and his mother would be ashamed too. And in the school yard—it was too awful to contemplate.

He began putting his weight in a stirrup when Gabilan was saddled, but he didn't throw his leg over the pony's back. That was forbidden until Thanksgiving.

Every afternoon he put the red saddle on the pony and cinched it tight. The pony was learning already to fill his stomach out unnaturally large while the cinching was going on, and then to let it down when the straps were fixed. Sometimes Jody led him up to the brush line and let him drink from the round green tub, and sometimes he led him up through the stubble-field to the hilltop from which it was possible to see the white town of Salinas and the geometric fields of the great valley, and the oak trees clipped by the sheep. Now and then they broke through the brush and came to little cleared circles so hedged in that the world was gone and only the sky and the circle of brush were left from the old life. Gabilan liked these trips and showed it by keeping his head very high and by quivering his nostrils with interest. When the two came back from an expedition they smelled of the sweet sage they had forced through.

Time dragged on toward Thanksgiving, but winter came fast. The clouds swept down and hung all day over the land and brushed the hilltops, and the winds blew shrilly at night. All day the dry oak leaves drifted down from the trees until they covered the ground, and yet the trees were unchanged.

Jody had wished it might not rain before Thanksgiving, but it did. The brown earth turned dark and the trees glistened. The cut ends of the stubble turned black with mildew; the haystacks grayed from exposure to the damp, and on the roofs the moss, which had been all summer as grey as lizards, turned a brilliant yellow-green. During the week of rain, Jody kept the pony in the box stall out of the dampness, except for a little time after school when he took him out for exercise and to drink at the water-trough in the upper corral. Not once did Gabilan get wet.

The wet weather continued until little new grass appeared. Jody walked to school dressed in a slicker and short rubber boots. At length one morning the sun came out brightly. Jody, at his work in the box stall, said to Billy Buck, "Maybe I'll leave Gabilan in the corral when I go to school today."

"Be good for him to be out in the sun," Billy assured him. "No animal likes to be cooped up too long. Your father and me are going back on the hill to clean the leaves out of the spring." Billy nodded and picked his teeth with one of his little straws.

"If the rain comes, though—" Jody suggested.

"Not likely to rain today. She's rained herself out." Billy pulled up his sleeves and snapped his arm bands. "If it comes on to rain—why a little rain don't hurt a horse."

"Well, if it does come on to rain, you put him in, will you, Billy? I'm scared he might get cold so I couldn't ride him when the time comes."

21

"Oh sure! I'll watch out for him if we get back in time. But it won't rain today."

And so Jody, when he went to school left Gabilan standing out in the corral.

Billy Buck wasn't wrong about many things. He couldn't be. But he was wrong about the weather that day, for a little after noon the clouds pushed over the hills and the rain began to pour down. Jody heard it start on the schoolhouse roof. He considered holding up one finger for permission to go to the outhouse and, once outside, running for home to put the pony in. Punishment would be prompt both at school and at home. He gave it up and took ease from Billy's assurance that rain couldn't hurt a horse. When school was finally out, he hurried home through the dark rain. The banks at the sides of the road spouted little jets of muddy water. The rain slanted and swirled under a cold and gusty wind. Jody dog-trotted home, slopping through the gravelly mud of the road.

From the top of the ridge he could see Gabilan standing miserably in the corral. The red coat was almost black, and streaked with water. He stood head down with his rump to the rain and wind. Jody arrived running and threw open the barn door and led the wet pony in by his forelock. Then he found a gunny sack and rubbed the soaked hair and rubbed the legs and ankles. Gabilan stood patiently, but he trembled in gusts like the wind.

When he had dried the pony as well as he could, Jody went up to the house and brought hot water down to the barn and soaked the grain in it. Gabilan was not very hungry. He nibbled at the hot mash, but he was not very much interested in it, and he still shivered now and then. A little steam rose from his damp back.

It was almost dark when Billy Buck and Carl Tiflin

came home. "When the rain started we put up at Ben Herche's place, and the rain never let up all afternoon," Carl Tiflin explained. Jody looked reproachfully at Billy Buck and Billy felt guilty.

"You said it wouldn't rain," Jody accused him.

Billy looked away. "It's hard to tell, this time of year," he said, but his excuse was lame. He had no right to be fallible, and he knew it.

"The pony got wet, got soaked through."

"Did you dry him off?"

"I rubbed him with a sack and I gave him hot grain." Billy nodded in agreement.

"Do you think he'll take cold, Billy?"

"A little rain never hurt anything," Billy assured him.

Jody's father joined the conversation then and lectured the boy a little. "A horse," he said, "isn't any lap-dog kind of thing." Carl Tiflin hated weakness and sickness, and he held a violent contempt for helplessness.

Jody's mother put a platter of steaks on the table and boiled potatoes and boiled squash, which clouded the room with their steam. They sat down to eat. Carl Tiflin still grumbled about weakness put into animals and men by too much coddling.

Billy Buck felt bad about his mistake. "Did you blanket him?" he asked.

"No. I couldn't find any blanket. I laid some sacks over his back."

"We'll go down and cover him up after we eat, then." Billy felt better about it then. When Jody's father had gone in to the fire and his mother was washing dishes, Billy found and lighted a lantern. He and Jody walked through the mud to the barn. The barn was dark and warm and sweet. The horses still munched their evening hay. "You hold the lantern!" Billy ordered. And he felt the pony's legs and tested the heat of the flanks. He put

23

his cheek against the pony's grey muzzle and then he rolled up the eyelids to look at the eyeballs and he lifted the lips to see the gums, and he put his fingers inside the ears. "He don't seem so chipper," Billy said. "I'll give him a rub-down."

Then Billy found a sack and rubbed the pony's legs violently and he rubbed the chest and the withers. Gabilan was strangely spiritless. He submitted patiently to the rubbing. At last Billy brought an old cotton comforter from the saddle-room, and threw it over the pony's back and tied it at neck and chest with string.

"Now he'll be all right in the morning," Billy said.

Jody's mother looked up when he got back to the house. "You're late up from bed," she said. She held his chin in her hard hand and brushed the tangled hair out of his eyes and she said, "Don't worry about the pony. He'll be all right. Billy's as good as any horse doctor in the country."

Jody hadn't known she could see his worry. He pulled gently away from her and knelt down in front of the fireplace until it burned his stomach. He scorched himself through and then went in to bed, but it was a hard thing to go to sleep. He awakened after what seemed a long time. The room was dark but there was a greyness in the window like that which precedes the dawn. He got up and found his overalls and searched for the legs, and then the clock in the other room struck two. He laid his clothes down and got back into bed. It was broad daylight when he awakened again. For the first time he had slept through the ringing of the triangle. He leaped up, flung on his clothes and went out of the door still buttoning his shirt. His mother looked after him for a moment and then went quietly back to her work. Her eyes were brooding and kind. Now and then her mouth smiled a little but without changing her eyes at all.

Jody ran on toward the barn. Halfway there he heard the sound he dreaded, the hollow rasping cough of a horse. He broke into a sprint then. In the barn he found Billy Buck with the pony. Billy was rubbing his legs with his strong thick hands. He looked up and smiled gaily. "He just took a little cold," Billy said. "We'll have him out of it in a couple of days."

Jody looked at the pony's face. The eyes were half closed and the lids thick and dry. In the eye corners a crust of hard mucus stuck. Gabilan's ears hung loosely sideways and his head was low. Jody put out his hand, but the pony did not move close to it. He coughed again and his whole body constricted with the effort. A little stream of thin fluid ran from his nostrils.

Jody looked back at Billy Buck. "He's awful sick, Billy."

"Just a little cold, like I said," Billy insisted. "You go get some breakfast and then go back to school. I'll take care of him."

"But you might have to do something else. You might leave him."

"No, I won't. I won't leave him at all. Tomorrow's Saturday. Then you can stay with him all day." Billy had failed again, and he felt badly about it. He had to cure the pony now.

Jody walked up to the house and took his place listlessly at the table. The eggs and bacon were cold and greasy, but he didn't notice it. He ate his usual amount. He didn't even ask to stay home from school. His mother pushed his hair back when she took his plate. "Billy'll take care of the pony," she assured him.

He moped through the whole day at school. He couldn't answer any questions nor read any words. He couldn't even tell anyone the pony was sick, for that might make him sicker. And when school was finally out he started home in dread. He walked slowly and let the other boys leave him. He wished he might continue walking and never arrive at the ranch.

Billy was in the barn, as he had promised, and the pony was worse. His eyes were almost closed now, and his breath whistled shrilly past an obstruction in his nose. A film covered that part of the eyes that was visible at all. It was doubtful whether the pony could see any more. Now and then he snorted, to clear his nose, and by the action seemed to plug it tighter. Jody looked dispiritedly at the pony's coat. The hair lay rough and unkempt and seemed to have lost all of its old luster. Billy stood quietly besides the stall. Jody hated to ask, but he had to know.

"Billy, is he—is he going to get well?"

Billy put his fingers between the bars under the pony's jaw and felt about. "Feel here," he said and he guided Jody's fingers to a large lump under the jaw. "When that gets bigger, I'll open it up and then he'll get better."

Jody looked quickly away, for he had heard about that lump. "What is it the matter with him?"

Billy didn't want to answer, but he had to. He couldn't be wrong three times. "Strangles," he said shortly, "but don't you worry about that. I'll pull him out of it. I've seen them get well when they were worse than Gabilan is. I'm going to steam him now. You can help."

"Yes," Jody said miserably. He followed Billy into the grain room and watched him make the steaming bag ready. It was a long canvas nose bag with straps to go over a horse's ears. Billy filled it one-third full of bran and then he added a couple of handfuls of dried hops. On top of the dry substance he poured a little carbolic acid and a little turpentine. 'I'll be mixing it all up while you run to the house for a kettle of boiling water," Billy said.

When Jody came back with the steaming kettle, Billy buckled the straps over Gabilan's head and fitted the bag tightly around his nose. Then through a little hole in the side of the bag he poured the boiling water on the mixture. The pony started away as a cloud of strong steam rose up, but then the soothing fumes crept through his nose and into his lungs, and the sharp steam began to clear out the nasal passages. He breathed loudly. His legs trembled in an ague, and his eyes closed against the biting cloud. Billy poured in more water and kept the steam rising for fifteen minutes. At last he set down the kettle and took the bag from Gabilan's nose. The pony looked better. He breathed freely, and his eyes were open wider than they had been.

"See how good it makes him feel," Billy said. "Now we'll wrap him up in the blanket again. Maybe he'll be nearly well by morning."

"I'll stay with him tonight," Jody suggested.

"No. Don't you do it. I'll bring my blankets down here and put them in the hay. You can stay tomorrow and steam him if he needs it."

The evening was falling when they went to the house for their supper. Jody didn't even realize that some one else had fed the chickens and filled the wood-box. He walked up past the house to the dark brush line and took a drink of water from the tub. The spring water was so cold that it stung his mouth and drove a shiver through him. The sky above the hills was still light. He saw a hawk flying so high that it caught the sun on its breast and shone like a spark. Two blackbirds were driving him down the sky, glittering as they attacked their enemy. In the west, the clouds were moving in to rain again.

Jody's father didn't speak at all while the family ate supper, but after Billy Buck had taken his blankets and gone to sleep in the barn, Carl Tiflin built a high fire in the fireplace and told stories. He told about the wild man who ran naked through the country and had a tail and ears like a horse, and he told about the rabbit-cats of Moro Cojo that hopped into the trees for birds. He revived the famous Maxwell brothers who found a vein of gold and hid the traces of it so carefully that they could never find it again.

Jody sat with his chin in his hands; his mouth worked nervously, and his father gradually became aware that he wasn't listening very carefully. "Isn't that funny?" he asked.

Jody laughed politely and said, "Yes, sir." His father was angry and hurt, then. He didn't tell any more stories. After a while, Jody took a lantern and went down to the barn. Billy Buck was asleep in the hay, and, except that his breath rasped a little in his lungs, the pony seemed to be much better. Jody stayed a little while, running his fingers over the red rough coat, and then he took up the lantern and went back to the house. When he was in bed, his mother came into the room.

"Have you enough covers on? It's getting winter."

"Yes, ma'am."

"Well, get some rest tonight." She hesitated to go out, stood uncertainly. "The pony will be all right," she said.

Jody was tired. He went to sleep quickly and didn't awaken until dawn. The triangle sounded, and Billy Buck came up from the barn before Jody could get out of the house.

"How is he?" Jody demanded.

Billy always wolfed his breakfast. "Pretty good. I'm going to open that lump this morning. Then he'll be better maybe."

After breakfast, Billy got out his best knife, one with a needle point. He whetted the shining blade a long time

28

on a little carborundum stone. He tried the point and the blade again and again on his calloused thumb-ball, and at last he tried it on his upper lip.

On the way to the barn, Jody noticed how the young grass was up and how the stubble was melting day by day into the new green crop of volunteer. It was a cold sunny morning.

As soon as he saw the pony, Jody knew he was worse. His eyes were closed and sealed shut with dried mucus. His head hung so low that his nose almost touched the straw of his bed. There was a little groan in each breath, a deep-seated, patient groan.

Billy lifted the weak head and made a quick slash with the knife. Jody saw the yellow pus run out. He held up the head while Billy swabbed out the wound with weak carbolic acid salve.

"Now he'll feel better," Billy assured him. "That yellow poison is what makes him sick."

Jody looked unbelieving at Billy Buck. "He's awful sick."

Billy thought a long time what to say. He nearly tossed off a careless assurance, but he saved himself in time. "Yes, he's pretty sick," he said at last. "I've seen worse ones get well. If he doesn't get pneumonia, we'll pull him through. You stay with him. If he gets worse, you can come and get me."

For a long time after Billy went away, Jody stood beside the pony, stroking him behind the ears. The pony didn't flip his head the way he had done when he was well. The groaning in his breathing was becoming more hollow.

Doubletree Mutt looked into the barn, his big tail waving provocatively, and Jody was so incensed at his health that he found a hard black clod on the floor and deliberately threw it. Doubletree Mutt went yelping away to nurse a bruised paw.

In the middle of the morning, Billy Buck came back and made another steam bag. Jody watched to see whether the pony improved this time as he had before. His breathing eased a little, but he did not raise his head.

The Saturday dragged on. Late in the afternoon Jody went to the house and brought his bedding down and made up a place to sleep in the hay. He didn't ask permission. He knew from the way his mother looked at him that she would let him do almost anything. That night he left a lantern burning on a wire over the box stall. Billy had told him to rub the pony's legs every little while.

At nine o'clock the wind sprang up and howled around the barn. And in spite of his worry, Jody grew sleepy. He got into his blankets and went to sleep, but the breathy groans of the pony sounded in his dreams. And in his sleep he heard a crashing noise which went on and on until it awakened him. The wind was rushing through the barn. He sprang up and looked down the lane of stalls. The barn door had blown open, and the pony was gone.

He caught the lantern and ran outside into the gale, and he saw Gabilan weakly shambling away into the darkness, head down, legs working slowly and mechanically. When Jody ran up and caught him by the forelock, he allowed himself to be led back and put into his stall. His groans were louder, and a fierce whistling came from his nose. Jody didn't sleep any more then. The hissing of the pony's breath grew louder and sharper.

He was glad when Billy Buck came in at dawn. Billy looked for a time at the pony as though he had never seen him before. He felt the ears and flanks. "Jody," he said, "I've got to do something you won't want to see. You run up to the house for a while."

Jody grabbed him fiercely by the forearm. "You're not going to shoot him?"

Billy patted his hand. "No. I'm going to open a little hole in his windpipe so he can breathe. His nose is filled up. When he gets well, we'll put a little brass button in the hole for him to breathe through."

Jody couldn't have gone away if he had wanted to. It was awful to see the red hide cut, but infinitely more terrible to know it was being cut and not to see it. "I'll stay right here," he said bitterly. "You sure you got to?"

"Yes. I'm sure. If you stay, you can hold his head. If it doesn't make you sick, that is."

The fine knife came out again and was whetted again just as carefully as it had been the first time. Jody held the pony's head up and the throat taut, while Billy felt up and down for the right place. Jody sobbed once as the bright knife point disappeared into the throat. The pony plunged weakly away and then stood still, trembling violently. The blood ran thickly out and up the knife and across Billy's hand and into his shirtsleeve. The sure square hand sawed out a round hole in the flesh, and the breath came bursting out of the hole, throwing a fine spray of blood. With the rush of oxygen, the pony took a sudden strength. He lashed out with his hind feet and tried to rear, but Jody held his head down while Billy mopped the new wound with carbolic salve. It was a good job. The blood stopped flowing and the air puffed out of the hole and sucked it in regularly with a little bubbling noise.

The rain brought in by the night wind began to fall on the barn roof. Then the triangle rang for breakfast. "You go up and eat while I wait," Billy said. "We've got to keep this hole from plugging up."

31

Jody walked slowly out of the barn. He was too dispirited to tell Billy how the barn door had blown open and let the pony out. He emerged into the wet grey morning and sloshed up to the house, taking a perverse pleasure in splashing through all the puddles. His mother fed him and put dry clothes on. She didn't question him. She seemed to know he couldn't answer questions. But when he was ready to go back to the barn she brought him a pan of steaming meal. "Give him this," she said.

But Jody did not take the pan. He said, "He won't eat anything," and ran out of the house. At the barn, Billy showed him how to fix a ball of cotton on a stick, with which to swab out the breathing hole when it became clogged with mucus.

Jody's father walked into the barn and stood with them in front of the stall. At length he turned to the boy. "Hadn't you better come with me? I'm going to drive over the hill." Jody shook his head. "You better come on, out of this," his father insisted.

Billy turned on him angrily. "Let him alone. It's his pony, isn't it?"

Carl Tiflin walked away without saying another word. His feelings were badly hurt.

All morning Jody kept the wound open and the air passing in and out freely. At noon the pony lay wearily down on his side and stretched his nose out.

Billy came back. "If you're going to stay with him tonight, you better take a little nap," he said. Jody went absently out of the barn. The sky had cleared to a hard thin blue. Everywhere the birds were busy with worms that had come to the damp surface of the ground.

Jody walked to the brush line and sat on the edge of the mossy tub. He looked down at the house and at the old bunkhouse and at the dark cypress tree. The place was familiar, but curiously changed. It wasn't itself any more, but a frame for things that were happening. A cold wind blew out of the east now, signifying that the rain was over for a little while. At his feet Jody could see the little arms of new weeds spreading out over the ground. In the mud about the spring were thousands of quail tracks.

Doubletree Mutt came sideways and embarrassed up through the vegetable patch, and Jody, remembering how he had thrown the clod, put his arm about the dog's neck and kissed him on his wide black nose. Doubletree Mutt sat still, as though he knew some solemn thing was happening. His big tail slapped the ground gravely. Jody pulled a swollen tick out of Mutt's neck and popped it dead between his thumb-nails. It was a nasty thing. He washed his hands in the cold spring water.

Except for the steady swish of the wind, the farm was very quiet. Jody knew his mother wouldn't mind if he didn't go in to eat his lunch. After a little while he went slowly back to the barn. Mutt crept into his own little house and whined softly to himself for a long time.

Billy Buck stood up from the box and surrendered the cotton swab. The pony still lay on his side and the wound in his throat bellowed in and out. When Jody saw how dry and dead the hair looked, he knew at last that there was no hope for the pony. He had seen the dead hair before on dogs and on cows, and it was a sure sign. He sat heavily on the box and let down the barrier of the box stall. For a long time he kept his eyes on the moving wound, and at last he dozed, and the afternoon passed quickly. Just before dark his mother brought a deep dish of stew and left it for him and went away. Jody ate a little of it, and, when it was dark, he set the lantern on the floor by the pony's head so he could watch the wound and keep it open. And he dozed again until the night chill awakened him. The wind was blowing fiercely, bringing the north cold with it. Jody brought a blanket from his bed in the hay and wrapped himself in it. Gabilan's breathing was quiet at last; the hole in his throat moved gently. The owls flew through the hayloft, shrieking and looking for mice. Jody put his hands down on his head and slept. In his sleep he was aware that the wind had increased. He heard it slamming about the barn.

It was daylight when he awakened. The barn door had swung open. The pony was gone. He sprang up and ran out into the morning light.

The pony's tracks were plain enough, dragging through the frostlike dew on the young grass, tired tracks with little lines between them where the hoofs had dragged. They headed for the brush line halfway up the ridge. Jody broke into a run and followed them. The sun shone on the sharp white quartz that stuck through the ground here and there. As he followed the plain trail, a shadow cut across in front of him. He looked up and saw a high circle of black buzzards, and the slowly revolving circle dropped lower and lower. The solemn birds soon disappeared over the ridge. Jody ran faster then, forced on by panic and rage. The trail entered the brush at last and followed a winding route among the tall sage bushes.

At the top of the ridge Jody was winded. He paused, puffing noisily. The blood pounded in his ears. Then he saw what he was looking for. Below, in one of the little clearings in the brush, lay the red pony. In the distance, Jody could see the legs moving slowly and convulsively. And in a circle around him stood the buzzards, waiting for the moment of death they know so well.

Jody leaped forward and plunged down the hill. The wet ground muffled his steps and the brush hid him. When he arrived, it was all over. The first buzzard sat on the pony's head and its beak had just risen dripping with dark eye fluid. Jody plunged into the circle like a cat. The black brotherhood arose in a cloud, but the big one on the pony's head was too late. As it hopped along to take off, Jody caught its wing tip and pulled it down. It was nearly as big as he was. The free wing crashed into his face with the force of a club, but he hung on. The claws fastened on his leg and the wing elbows battered his head on either side. Jody groped blindly with his free hand. His fingers found the neck of the struggling bird. The red eyes looked into his face, calm and fearless and fierce; the naked head turned from side to side. Then the beak opened and vomited a stream of putrified fluid. Jody brought up his knee and fell on the great bird. He held the neck to the ground with one hand while his other found a piece of sharp white quartz. The first blow broke the beak sideways and black blood spurted from the twisted, leathery mouth corners. He struck again and missed. The red fearless eyes still looked at him, impersonal and unafraid and detached. He struck again and again, until the buzzard lay dead, until its head was a red pulp. He was still beating the dead bird when Billy Buck pulled him off, and held him tightly to calm his shaking.

Carl Tiflin wiped the blood from the boy's face with a red bandana. Jody was limp and quiet now. His father moved the buzzard with his toe. "Jody," he explained, "the buzzard didn't kill the pony. Don't you know that?"

"I know it," Jody said wearily.

It was Billy Buck who was angry. He had lifted Jody in his arms, and had turned to carry him home. But he turned back on Carl Tiflin. " 'Course he knows it," Billy said furiously, "Jesus Christ! man, can't you see how he'd feel about it?"

II. THE GREAT MOUNTAINS

IN THE humming heat of a midsummer afternoon the little boy Jody listlessly looked about the ranch for something to do. He had been to the barn, had thrown rocks at the swallows' nests under the eaves until every one of the little mud houses broke open and dropped its lining of straw and dirty feathers. Then at the ranch house he baited a rat trap with stale cheese and set it where Doubletree Mutt, that good big dog, would get his nose snapped. Jody was not moved by an impulse of cruelty; he was bored with the long hot afternoon. Doubletree Mutt put his stupid nose in the trap and got it smacked, and shrieked with agony and limped away with blood on his nostrils. No matter where he was hurt, Mutt limped. It was just a way he had. Once when he was young, Mutt got caught in a coyote trap, and always after that he limped, even when he was scolded.

When Mutt yelped, Jody's mother called from inside the house, "Jody! Stop torturing that dog and find something to do."

Jody felt mean then, so he threw a rock at Mutt. Then he took his slingshot from the porch and walked up toward the brush line to try to kill a bird. It was a good slingshot, with store-bought rubbers, but while Jody had often shot at birds, he had never hit one. He walked up through the vegetable patch, kicking his bare toes into the dust. And on the way he found the perfect slingshot stone, round and slightly flattened and heavy enough to carry through the air. He fitted it into the leather pouch of his weapon and proceeded to the brush line. His eyes narrowed, his mouth worked strenuously; for the first time that afternoon he was intent. In the shade of the sagebrush the little birds were working, scratching in the leaves, flying restlessly a few feet and scratching again. Jody pulled back the rubbers of the sling and advanced cautiously. One little thrush paused and looked at him and crouched, ready to fly. Jody sidled nearer, moving one foot slowly after the other. When he was twenty feet away, he carefully raised the sling and aimed. The stone whizzed; the thrush started up and flew right into it. And down the little bird went with a broken head. Jody ran to it and picked it up.

"Well, I got you," he said.

The bird looked much smaller dead than it had alive. Jody felt a little mean pain in his stomach, so he took out his pocket-knife and cut off the bird's head. Then he disemboweled it, and took off its wings; and finally he threw all the pieces into the brush. He didn't care about the bird, or its life, but he knew what older people would say if they had seen him kill it; he was ashamed because of their potential opinion. He decided to forget the whole thing as quickly as he could, and never to mention it.

The hills were dry at this season, and the wild grass was golden, but where the spring-pipe filled the round tub and the tub spilled over, there lay a stretch of fine green grass, deep and sweet and moist. Jody drank from the mossy tub and washed the bird's blood from his hands in cold water. Then he lay on his back in the grass and looked up at the dumpling summer clouds. By closing one eye and destroying perspective he brought them down within reach so that he could put up his fingers and stroke them. He helped the gentle wind push them down the sky; it seemed to him that they went faster for his help. One fat white cloud he helped clear to the mountain rims and pressed it firmly over, out of sight. Jody wondered what it was seeing, then. He sat up the better to look at the great mountains where they went piling back, growing darker and more savage until they finished with one jagged ridge, high up against the west. Curious secret mountains; he thought of the little he knew about them.

"What's on the other side?" he asked his father once.

"More mountains, I guess. Why?"

"And on the other side of them?"

"More mountains. Why?"

"More mountains on and on?"

"Well, no. At last you come to the ocean."

"But what's in the mountains?"

"Just cliffs and brush and rocks and dryness."

"Were you ever there?"

"No."

"Has anybody ever been there?"

"A few people, I guess. It's dangerous, with cliffs and things. Why, I've read there's more unexplored country in the mountains of Monterey County than any place in the United States." His father seemed proud that this should be so.

"And at last the ocean?"

"At last the ocean."

"But," the boy insisted, "but in between? No one knows?"

"Oh, a few people do, I guess. But there's nothing there to get. And not much water. Just rocks and cliffs and greasewood. Why?"

"It would be good to go."

"What for? There's nothing there."

Jody knew something was there, something very wonderful because it wasn't known, something secret and mysterious. He could feel within himself that this was so.

He said to his mother, "Do you know what's in the big mountains?"

She looked at him and then back at the ferocious range, and she said, "Only the bear, I guess."

"What bear?"

"Why the one that went over the mountain to see what he could see."

Jody questioned Billy Buck, the ranch hand, about the possibility of ancient cities lost in the mountains, but Billy agreed with Jody's father.

"It ain't likely," Billy said. "There'd be nothing to eat unless a kind of people that can eat rocks live there."

That was all the information Jody ever got, and it made the mountains dear to him, and terrible. He thought often of the miles of ridge after ridge until at last there was the sea. When the peaks were pink in the morning they invited him among them: and when the sun had gone over the edge in the evening and the mountains were a purple-like despair, then Jody was afraid of them; then they were so impersonal and aloof that their very imperturbability was a threat.

Now he turned his head toward the mountains of the east, the Gabilans, and they were jolly mountains, with hill ranches in their creases, and with pine trees growing on the crests. People lived there, and battles had been fought against the Mexicans on the slopes. He looked back for an instant at the Great Ones and shivered a little at the contrast. The foothill cup of the home ranch below him was sunny and safe. The house gleamed with white light and the barn was brown and warm. The red cows on the farther hill ate their way slowly toward the north. Even the dark cypress tree by the bunkhouse was usual and safe. The chickens scratched about in the dust of the farmyard with quick waltzing steps.

Then a moving figure caught Jody's eye. A man walked slowly over the brow of the hill, on the road from Salinas, and he was headed toward the house. Jody stood up and moved down toward the house too, for if someone was coming, he wanted to be there to see. By the time the boy had got to the house the walking man was only halfway down the road, a lean man, very straight in the shoulders. Jody could tell he was old only because his heels struck the ground with hard jerks. As he approached nearer, Jody saw that he was dressed in blue jeans and in a coat of the same material. He wore clodhopper shoes and an old flat-brimmed Stetson hat. Over his shoulder he carried a gunny sack, lumpy and full. In a few moments he had trudged close enough so that his face could be seen. And his face was as dark as dried beef. A mustache, blue-white against the dark skin, hovered over his mouth, and his hair was white, too, where it showed at his neck. The skin of his face had shrunk back against the skull until it defined bone, not flesh, and made the nose and chin seem sharp and fragile. The eyes were large and deep and dark, with eyelids stretched tightly over them. Irises and pupils were one, and very black, but the eyeballs were brown. There were no wrinkles in the face at all. This old man wore a blue denim coat buttoned to the throat with brass buttons, as all men do who wear no shirts. Out of the sleeves came strong bony wrists and hands gnarled and knotted and hard as peach branches. The nails were flat and blunt and shiny.

The old man drew close to the gate and swung down his sack when he confronted Jody. His lips fluttered a little and a soft impersonal voice came from between them.

"Do you live here?"

Jody was embarrassed. He turned and looked at the house, and he turned back and looked toward the barn where his father and Billy Buck were. "Yes," he said, when no help came from either direction.

"I have come back," the old man said. "I am Gitano, and I have come back."

Jody could not take all this responsibility. He turned abruptly, and ran into the house for help, and the screen door banged after him. His mother was in the kitchen poking out the clogged holes of a colander with a hairpin, and biting her lower lip with concentration.

"It's an old man," Jody cried excitedly. "It's an old *paisano* man, and he says he's come back."

His mother put down the colander and stuck the hairpin behind the sink board. "What's the matter now?" she asked patiently.

"It's an old man outside. Come on out."

"Well, what does he want?" She untied the strings of her apron and smoothed her hair with her fingers.

"I don't know. He came walking."

His mother smoothed down her dress and went out, and Jody followed her. Gitano had not moved.

"Yes?" Mrs. Tiflin asked.

Gitano took off his old black hat and held it with both hands in front of him. He repeated, "I am Gitano, and I have come back."

"Come back? Back where?"

Gitano's whole straight body leaned forward a little. His right hand described the circle of the hills, the sloping fields and the mountains, and ended at his hat again. "Back to the rancho. I was born here, and my father, too."

"Here?" she demanded. "This isn't an old place."

"No, there," he said, pointing to the western ridge. "On the other side there, in a house that is gone."

41

At last she understood. "The old 'dobe that's washed almost away, you mean?"

"Yes, *señora*. When the rancho broke up they put no more lime on the 'dobe, and the rains washed it down."

Jody's mother was silent for a little, and curious homesick thoughts ran through her mind, but quickly she cleared them out. "And what do you want here now, Gitano?"

"I will stay here," he said quietly, "until I die."

"But we don't need an extra man here."

"I can not work hard any more, *señora*. I can milk a cow, feed chickens, cut a little wood; no more. I will stay here." He indicated the sack on the ground beside him. "Here are my things."

She turned to Jody. "Run down to the barn and call your father."

Jody dashed away, and he returned with Carl Tiflin and Billy Buck behind him. The old man was standing as he had been, but he was resting now. His whole body had sagged into a timeless repose.

"What is it?" Carl Tiflin asked. "What's Jody so excited about?"

Mrs. Tiflin motioned to the old man. "He wants to stay here. He wants to do a little work and stay here."

"Well, we can't have him. We don't need any more men. He's too old. Billy does everything we need."

They had been talking over him as though he did not exist, and now, suddenly, they both hesitated and looked at Gitano and were embarrassed.

He cleared his throat. "I am too old to work. I come back where I was born."

"You weren't born here," Carl said sharply.

"No. In the 'dobe house over the hill. It was all one rancho before you came."

"In the mud house that's all melted down?"

"Yes, I and my father. I will stay here now on the rancho."

"I tell you you won't stay," Carl said angrily. "I don't need an old man. This isn't a big ranch. I can't afford food and doctor bills for an old man. You must have relatives and friends. Go to them. It is like begging to come to strangers."

"I was born here," Gitano said patiently and inflexibly.

Carl Tiflin didn't like to be cruel, but he felt he must. "You can eat here tonight," he said. "You can sleep in the little room of the old bunkhouse. We'll give you your breakfast in the morning, and then you'll have to go along. Go to your friends. Don't come to die with strangers."

Gitano put on his black hat and stooped for the sack. "Here are my things," he said.

Carl turned away. "Come on, Billy, we'll finish down at the barn. Jody, show him the little room in the bunkhouse."

He and Billy turned back toward the barn. Mrs. Tiflin went into the house, saying over her shoulder, "I'll send some blankets down."

Gitano looked questioningly at Jody. "I'll show you where it is," Jody said.

There was a cot with a shuck mattress, an apple box holding a tin lantern, and a backless rocking-chair in the little room of the bunkhouse. Gitano laid his sack carefully on the floor and sat down on the bed. Jody stood shyly in the room, hesitating to go. At last he said,

"Did you come out of the big mountains?"

Gitano shook his head slowly. "No, I worked down the Salinas Valley."

The afternoon thought would not let Jody go. "Did you ever go into the big mountains back there?"

The old dark eyes grew fixed, and their light turned inward on the years that were living in Gitano's head. "Once—when I was a little boy. I went with my father."

"Way back, clear into the mountains?"

"Yes."

"What was there?" Jody cried. "Did you see any people or any houses?"

"No."

"Well, what was there?"

Gitano's eyes remained inward. A little wrinkled strain came between his brows.

"What did you see in there?" Jody repeated.

"I don't know," Gitano said. "I don't remember."

"Was it terrible and dry?"

"I don't remember."

In his excitement, Jody had lost his shyness. "Don't you remember anything about it?"

Gitano's mouth opened for a word, and remained open while his brain sought the word. "I think it was quiet— I think it was nice."

Gitano's eyes seemed to have found something back in the years, for they grew soft and a little smile seemed to come and go in them.

"Didn't you ever go back in the mountains again?" Jody insisted.

"No."

"Didn't you ever want to?"

But now Gitano's face became impatient. "No," he said in a tone that told Jody he didn't want to talk about it any more. The boy was held by a curious fascination. He didn't want to go away from Gitano. His shyness returned.

"Would you like to come down to the barn and see the stock?" he asked.

Gitano stood up and put on his hat and prepared to follow.

It was almost evening now. They stood near the watering trough while the horses sauntered in from the hillsides for an evening drink. Gitano rested his big twisted hands on the top rail of the fence. Five horses came down and drank, and then stood about, nibbling at the dirt or rubbing their sides against the polished wood of the fence. Long after they had finished drinking an old horse appeared over the brow of the hill and came painfully down. It had long yellow teeth; its hoofs were flat and sharp as spades, and its ribs and hip-bones jutted out under its skin. It hobbled up to the trough and drank water with a loud sucking noise.

"That's old Easter," Jody explained. "That's the first horse my father ever had. He's thirty years old." He looked up into Gitano's old eyes for some response.

"No good any more," Gitano said.

Jody's father and Billy Buck came out of the barn and walked over.

"Too old to work," Gitano repeated. "Just eats and pretty soon dies."

Carl Tiflin caught the last words. He hated his brutality toward old Gitano, and so he became brutal again.

"It's a shame not to shoot Easter," he said. "It'd save him a lot of pains and rheumatism." He looked secretly at Gitano, to see whether he noticed the parallel, but the big bony hands did not move, nor did the dark eyes turn from the horse. "Old things ought to be put out of their misery," Jody's father went on. "One shot, a big noise, one big pain in the head maybe, and that's all. That's better than stiffness and sore teeth."

Billy Buck broke in. "They got a right to rest after they worked all their life. Maybe they like to just walk around."

45

Carl had been looking steadily at the skinny horse. "You can't imagine now what Easter used to look like," he said softly. "High neck, deep chest, fine barrel. He could jump a five-bar gate in stride. I won a flat race on him when I was fifteen years old. I could of got two hundred dollars for him any time. You wouldn't think how pretty he was." He checked himself, for he hated softness. "But he ought to be shot now," he said.

"He's got a right to rest," Billy Buck insisted.

Jody's father had a humorous thought. He turned to Gitano. "If ham and eggs grew on a side-hill I'd turn you out to pasture too," he said. "But I can't afford to pasture you in my kitchen."

He laughed to Billy Buck about it as they went on toward the house. "Be a good thing for all of us if ham and eggs grew on the side-hills."

Jody knew how his father was probing for a place to hurt Gitano. He had been probed often. His father knew every place in the boy where a word would fester.

"He's only talking," Jody said. "He didn't mean it about shooting Easter. He likes Easter. That was the first horse he ever owned."

The sun sank behind the high mountains as they stood there, and the ranch was hushed. Gitano seemed to be more at home in the evening. He made a curious sharp sound with his lips and stretched one of his hands over the fence. Old Easter moved stiffly to him, and Gitano rubbed the lean neck under the mane.

"You like him?" Jody asked softly.

"Yes—but he's no damn good."

The triangle sounded at the ranch house. "That's supper," Jody cried. "Come on up to supper."

As they walked up toward the house Jody noticed again that Gitano's body was as straight as that of a young man. Only by a jerkiness in his movements and by the scuffling of his heels could it be seen that he was old.

The turkeys were flying heavily into the lower branches of the cypress tree by the bunkhouse. A fat sleek ranch cat walked across the road carrying a rat so large that its tail dragged on the ground. The quail on the side-hills were still sounding the clear water call.

Jody and Gitano came to the back steps and Mrs. Tiflin looked out through the screen door at them.

"Come running, Jody. Come in to supper, Gitano."

Carl and Billy Buck had started to eat at the long oilcloth-covered table. Jody slipped into his chair without moving it, but Gitano stood holding his hat until Carl looked up and said, "Sit down, sit down. You might as well get your belly full before you go on." Carl was afraid he might relent and let the old man stay, and so he continued to remind himself that this couldn't be.

Gitano laid his hat on the floor and diffidently sat down. He wouldn't reach for food. Carl had to pass it to him. "Here, fill yourself up." Gitano ate very slowly, cutting tiny pieces of meat and arranging little pats of mashed potato on his plate.

The situation would not stop worrying Carl Tiflin. "Haven't you got any relatives in this part of the country?" he asked.

Gitano answered with some pride, "My brother-in-law is in Monterey. I have cousins there, too."

"Well, you can go and live there, then."

"I was born here," Gitano said in gentle rebuke.

Jody's mother came in from the kitchen, carrying a large bowl of tapioca pudding.

Carl chuckled to her, "Did I tell you what I said to him? I said if ham and eggs grew on the side-hills I'd put him out to pasture, like old Easter."

Gitano stared unmoved at his plate.

47

"It's too bad he can't stay," said Mrs. Tiflin.

"Now don't you start anything," Carl said crossly.

When they had finished eating, Carl and Billy Buck and Jody went into the living-room to sit for a while, but Gitano, without a word of farewell or thanks, walked through the kitchen and out the back door. Jody sat and secretly watched his father. He knew how mean his father felt.

"This country's full of these old *paisanos*," Carl said to Billy Buck.

"They're damn good men," Billy defended them. "They can work older than white men. I saw one of them a hundred and five years old, and he could still ride a horse. You don't see any white men as old as Gitano walking twenty or thirty miles."

"Oh, they're tough all right," Carl agreed. "Say, are you standing up for him too? Listen, Billy," he explained, "I'm having a hard enough time keeping this ranch out of the Bank of Italy without taking on anybody else to feed. You know that, Billy."

"Sure, I know," said Billy. "If you was rich, it'd be different."

"That's right, and it isn't like he didn't have relatives to go to. A brother-in-law and cousins right in Monterey. Why should I worry about him?"

Jody sat quietly listening, and he seemed to hear Gitano's gentle voice and its unanswerable, "But I was born here." Gitano was mysterious like the mountains. There were ranges back as far as you could see, but behind the last range piled up against the sky there was a great unknown country. And Gitano was an old man, until you got to the dull dark eyes. And in behind them was some unknown thing. He didn't ever say enough to let you guess what was inside, under the eyes. Jody felt himself irresistibly drawn toward the bunkhouse. He

48

slipped from his chair while his father was talking and he went out the door without making a sound.

The night was very dark and far-off noises carried in clearly. The hamebells of a wood team sounded from way over the hill on the country road. Jody picked his way across the dark yard. He could see a light through the window of the little room of the bunkhouse. Because the night was secret he walked quietly up to the window and peered in. Gitano sat in the rocking-chair and his back was toward the window. His right arm moved slowly back and forth in front of him. Jody pushed the door open and walked in. Gitano jerked upright and, seizing a piece of deerskin, he tried to throw it over the thing in his lap, but the skin slipped away. Jody stood overwhelmed by the thing in Gitano's hand, a lean and lovely rapier with a golden basket hilt. The blade was like a thin ray of dark light. The hilt was pierced and intricately carved.

"What is it?" Jody demanded.

Gitano only looked at him with resentful eyes, and he picked up the fallen deerskin and firmly wrapped the beautiful blade in it.

Jody put out his hand. "Can't I see it?"

Gitano's eyes smoldered angrily and he shook his head.

"Where'd you get it? Where'd it come from?"

Now Gitano regarded his profoundly, as though he pondered. "I got it from my father."

"Well, where'd he get it?"

Gitano looked down at the long deerskin parcel in his hand. "I don't know?"

"Didn't he ever tell you?"

"No."

"What do you do with it?"

Gitano looked slightly surprised. "Nothing. I just keep it."

"Can't I see it again?"

The old man slowly unwrapped the shining blade and let the lamplight slip along it for a moment. Then he wrapped it up again. "You go now. I want to go to bed." He blew out the lamp almost before Jody had closed the door.

As he went back toward the house, Jody knew one thing more sharply than he had ever known anything. He must never tell anyone about the rapier. It would be a dreadful thing to tell anyone about it, for it would destroy some fragile structure of truth. It was a truth that might be shattered by division.

On the way across the dark yard Jody passed Billy Buck. "They're wondering where you are," Billy said.

Jody slipped into the living-room, and his father turned to him. "Where have you been?"

"I just went out to see if I caught any rats in my new trap."

"It's time you went to bed," his father said.

Jody was first at the breakfast table in the morning. Then his father came in, and last, Billy Buck. Mrs. Tiflin looked in from the kitchen.

"Where's the old man, Billy?" she asked.

"I guess he's out walking," Billy said. "I looked in his room and he wasn't there."

"Maybe he started early to Monterey," said Carl. "It's a long walk."

"No," Billy explained. "His sack is in the little room."

After breakfast Jody walked down to the bunkhouse. Flies were flashing about in the sunshine. The ranch seemed especially quiet this morning. When he was sure no one was watching him, Jody went into the little room, and looked into Gitano's sack. An extra pair of long cotton underwear was there, an extra pair of jeans and three pairs of worn socks. Nothing else was in the sack.

A sharp loneliness fell on Jody. He walked slowly back toward the house. His father stood on the porch talking to Mrs. Tiflin.

"I guess old Easter's dead at last," he said. "I didn't see him come down to water with the other horses."

In the middle of the morning Jess Taylor from the ridge ranch rode down.

"You didn't sell that old gray crowbait of yours, did you, Carl?"

"No, of course not. Why?"

"Well," Jess said. "I was out this morning early, and I saw a funny thing. I saw an old man on an old horse, no saddle, only a piece of rope for a bridle. He wasn't on the road at all. He was cutting right up straight through the brush. I think he had a gun. At least I saw something shine in his hand."

"That's old Gitano," Carl Tiflin said. "I'll see if any of my guns are missing." He stepped into the house for a second. "Nope, all here. Which way was he heading, Jess?"

"Well, that's the funny thing. He was heading straight back into the mountains."

Carl laughed. "They never get too old to steal," he said. "I guess he stole old Easter."

"Want to go after him, Carl?"

"Hell no, just save me burying that horse. I wonder where he got the gun. I wonder what he wants back there."

Jody walked up through the vegetable patch, toward the brush line. He looked searchingly at the towering mountains—ridge after ridge after ridge until at last there was the ocean. For a moment he thought he could see a black speck crawling up the farthest ridge. Jody thought of the rapier and of Gitano. And he thought of the great mountains. A longing caressed him, and it was so sharp that he wanted to cry to get it out of his breast. He lay down in the green grass near the round tub at the brush line. He covered his eyes with his crossed arms and lay there a long time, and he was full of a nameless sorrow.

III. THE PROMISE

IN A mid-afternoon of spring, the little boy Jody walked martially along the brush-lined road toward his home ranch. Banging his knee against the golden lard bucket he used for school lunch, he contrived a good bass drum, while his tongue fluttered sharply against the teeth to fill in snare drums and occasional trumpets. Some time back the other members of the squad that walked so smartly from the school had turned into the various little canyons and taken the wagon roads to their own home ranches. Now Jody marched seemingly alone, with high-lifted knees and pounding feet; but behind him there was a phantom army with great flags and swords, silent but deadly.

The afternoon was green and gold with spring. Underneath the spread branches of the oaks the plants grew pale and tall, and on the hills the feed was smooth and thick. The sagebrushes shone with new silver leaves and the oaks wore hoods of golden green. Over the hills there hung such a green odor that the horses on the flats galloped madly, and then stopped, wondering; lambs, and even old sheep jumped in the air unexpectedly and landed on stiff legs, and went on eating; young clumsy calves butted their heads together and drew back and butted again.

As the grey and silent army marched past, led by Jody, the animals stopped their feeding and their play and watched it go by.

Suddenly Jody stopped. The grey army halted, bewildered and nervous. Jody went down on his knees. The army stood in long uneasy ranks for a moment, and then, with a soft sigh of sorrow, rose up in a faint grey mist and disappeared. Jody had seen the thorny crown of a horny-toad moving under the dust of the road. His grimy hand went out and grasped the spiked halo and held firmly while the little beast struggled. Then Jody turned the horny-toad over, exposing its pale gold stomach. With a gentle forefinger he stroked the throat and chest until the horny-toad relaxed, until its eyes closed and it lay languorous and asleep.

Jody opened his lunch pail and deposited the first game inside. He moved on now, his knees bent slightly, his shoulders crouched; his bare feet were wise and silent. In his right hand there was a long grey rifle. The brush along the road stirred restively under a new and unexpected population of grey tigers and grey bears. The hunting was very good, for by the time Jody reached the fork of the road where the mail box stood on a post, he had captured two more horny-toads, four little grass lizards, a blue snake, sixteen yellow-winged grasshoppers and a brown damp newt from under a rock. This assortment scrabbled unhappily against the tin of the lunch bucket.

At the road fork the rifle evaporated and the tigers and bears melted from the hillsides. Even the moist and uncomfortable creatures in the lunch pail ceased to exist, for the little red metal flag was up on the mail box, signifying that some postal matter was inside. Jody set his pail on the ground and opened the letter box. There was a Montgomery Ward catalog and a copy of the *Salinas Weekly Journal*. He slammed the box, picked up his lunch pail and trotted over the ridge and down into the cup of the ranch. Past the barn he ran, and past the used-up haystack and the bunkhouse and the cypress tree. He banged through the front screen door of the ranch house calling, "Ma'am, ma'am, there's a catalog."

Mrs. Tiflin was in the kitchen spooning clabbered milk into a cotton bag. She put down her work and rinsed her hands under the tap. "Here in the kitchen, Jody. Here I am."

He ran in and clattered his lunch pail on the sink. "Here it is. Can I open the catalog, ma'am?"

Mrs. Tiflin took up the spoon again and went back to her cottage cheese. "Don't lose it, Jody. Your father will want to see it." She scraped the last of the milk into the bag. "Oh, Jody, your father wants to see you before you go to your chores." She waved a cruising fly from the cheese bag.

Jody closed the new catalog in alarm. "Ma'am?"

"Why don't you ever listen? I say your father wants to see you."

The boy laid the catalog gently on the sink board. "Do you—is it something I did?"

Mrs. Tiflin laughed. "Always a bad conscience. What did you do?"

"Nothing, ma'am," he said lamely. But he couldn't remember, and besides it was impossible to know what action might later be construed as a crime.

His mother hung the full bag on a nail where it could drip into the sink. "He just said he wanted to see you when you got home. He's somewhere down by the barn."

Jody turned and went out the back door. Hearing his mother open the lunch pail and then gasp with rage, a memory stabbed him and he trotted away toward the barn, conscientiously not hearing the angry voice that called him from the house.

Carl Tiflin and Billy Buck, the ranch hand, stood against the lower pasture fence. Each man rested one foot on the lowest bar and both elbows on the top bar. They were talking slowly and aimlessly. In the pasture half a dozen horses nibbled contentedly at the sweet grass. The mare, Nellie, stood backed up against the gate, rubbing her buttocks on the heavy post.

Jody sidled uneasily near. He dragged one foot to give an impression of great innocence and nonchalance. When he arrived beside the men he put one foot on the lowest fence rail, rested his elbows on the second bar and looked into the pasture too. The two men glanced sideways at him.

"I wanted to see you," Carl said in the stern tone he reserved for children and animals.

"Yes, sir," said Jody guiltily.

"Billy, here, says you took good care of the pony before it died."

No punishment was in the air. Jody grew bolder. "Yes, sir, I did."

"Billy says you have a good patient hand with horses."

Jody felt a sudden warm friendliness for the ranch hand.

Billy put in, "He trained that pony as good as anybody I ever seen."

Then Carl Tiflin came gradually to the point. "If you could have another horse would you work for it?"

Jody shivered. "Yes, sir."

"Well, look here, then. Billy says the best way for you to be a good hand with horses is to raise a colt."

"It's the *only* good way," Billy interrupted.

"Now, look here, Jody," continued Carl. "Jess Taylor, up to the ridge ranch, has a fair stallion, but it'll cost five dollars. I'll put up the money, but you'll have to work it out all summer. Will you do that?"

Jody felt that his insides were shriveling. "Yes, sir," he said softly.

"And no complaining? And no forgetting when you're told to do something?"

"Yes, sir."

"Well, all right, then. Tomorrow morning you take Nellie up to the ridge ranch and get her bred. You'll have to take care of her, too, till she throws the colt."

"Yes, sir."

"You better get to the chickens and the wood now."

Jody slid away. In passing behind Billy Buck he very nearly put out his hand to touch the blue-jeaned legs. His shoulders swayed a little with maturity and importance.

He went to his work with unprecedented seriousness. This night he did not dump the can of grain to the chickens so that they had to leap over each other and struggle to get it. No, he spread the wheat so far and so carefully that the hens couldn't find some of it at all. And in the house, after listening to his mother's despair over boys who filled their lunch pails with slimy, suffocated reptiles, and bugs, he promised never to do it again. Indeed, Jody felt that all such foolishness was lost in the past. He was far too grown up ever to put horny-toads in his lunch pail any more. He carried in so much wood and built such a high structure with it that his mother walked in fear of an avalanche of oak. When he was done, when he had gathered eggs that had remained hidden for weeks, Jody walked down again past the cypress tree, and past the bunkhouse toward the pasture. A fat warty toad that looked out at him from under the watering troughs had no emotional effect on him at all.

Carl Tiflin and Billy Buck were not in sight, but from a metallic ringing on the other side of the barn Jody knew that Billy Buck was just starting to milk a cow.

The other horses were eating toward the upper end of the pasture, but Nellie continued to rub herself nervously against the post. Jody walked slowly near, saying, "So, girl, so-o, Nellie." The mare's ears went back naughtily and her lips drew away from her yellow teeth. She turned her head around; her eyes were glazed and mad. Jody climbed to the top of the fence and hung his feet over and looked paternally down on the mare.

The evening hovered while he sat there. Bats and nighthawks flicked about. Billy Buck, walking toward the house carrying a full milk bucket, saw Jody and stopped. "It's a long time to wait," he said gently. "You'll get awful tired waiting."

"No I won't, Billy. How long will it be?"

"Nearly a year."

"Well, I won't get tired."

The triangle at the house rang stridently. Jody climbed down from the fence and walked to supper beside Billy Buck. He even put out his hand and took hold of the milk bucket to help carry it.

The next morning after breakfast Carl Tiflin folded a five-dollar bill in a piece of newspaper and pinned the package in the bib pocket of Jody's overalls. Billy Buck haltered the mare Nellie and led her out of the pasture.

"Be careful now," he warned. "Hold her up short here so she can't bite you. She's crazy as a coot."

Jody took hold of the halter leather itself and started up the hill toward the ridge ranch with Nellie skittering and jerking behind him. In the pasturage along the road the wild oat heads were just clearing their scabbards. The warm morning sun shone on Jody's back so sweetly that he was forced to take a serious stiff-legged hop now and then in spite of his maturity. On the fences the shiny blackbirds with red epaulets clicked their dry call. The meadowlarks sang like water, and the wild doves, concealed among the bursting leaves of the oaks, made a sound of restrained grieving. In the fields the rabbits sat sunning themselves, with only their forked ears showing above the grass heads.

After an hour of steady uphill walking, Jody turned into a narrow road that led up a steeper hill to the ridge ranch. He could see the red roof of the barn sticking up above the oak trees, and he could hear a dog barking unemotionally near the house.

Suddenly Nellie jerked back and nearly freed herself. From the direction of the barn Jody heard a shrill whistling scream and a splintering of wood, and then a man's voice shouting. Nellie reared and whinnied. When Jody held to the halter rope she ran at him with bared teeth. He dropped his hold and scuttled out of the way, into the brush. The high scream came from the oaks again, and Nellie answered it. With hoofs battering the ground the stallion appeared and charged down the hill trailing a broken halter rope. His eyes glittered feverishly. His stiff, erected nostrils were as red as flame. His black, sleek hide shone in the sunlight. The stallion came on so fast that he couldn't stop when he reached the mare. Nellie's ears went back; she whirled and kicked at him as he went by. The stallion spun around and reared. He struck the mare with his front hoof, and while she staggered under the blow, his teeth raked her neck and drew an ooze of blood.

Instantly Nellie's mood changed. She became coquettishly feminine. She nibbled his arched neck with her lips. She edged around and rubbed her shoulder against his shoulder. Jody stood half-hidden in the brush and watched. He heard the step of a horse behind him, but before he could turn, a hand caught him by the overall straps and lifted him off the ground. Jess Taylor sat the boy behind him on the horse.

"You might have got killed," he said. "Sundog's a

mean devil sometimes. He busted his rope and went right through a gate."

Jody sat quietly, but in a moment he cried, "He'll hurt her, he'll kill her. Get him away!"

Jess chuckled. "She'll be all right. Maybe you'd better climb off and go up to the house for a little. You could get maybe a piece of pie up there."

But Jody shook his head. "She's mine, and the colt's going to be mine. I'm going to raise it up."

Jess nodded. "Yes, that's a good thing. Carl has good sense sometimes."

In a little while the danger was over. Jess lifted Jody down and then caught the stallion by its broken halter rope. And he rode ahead, while Jody followed, leading Nellie.

It was only after he had unpinned and handed over the five dollars, and after he had eaten two pieces of pie, that Jody started for home again. And Nellie followed docilely after him. She was so quiet that Jody climbed on a stump and rode her most of the way home.

The five dollars his father had advanced reduced Jody to peonage for the whole late spring and summer. When the hay was cut he drove a rake. He led the horse that pulled on the Jackson-fork tackle, and when the baler came he drove the circling horse that put pressure on the bales. In addition, Carl Tiflin taught him to milk and put a cow under his care, so that a new chore was added night and morning.

The bay mare Nellie quickly grew complacent. As she walked about the yellowing hillsides or worked at easy tasks, her lips were curled in a perpetual fatuous smile. She moved slowly, with the calm importance of an empress. When she was put to a team, she pulled steadily and unemotionally. Jody went to see her every day. He studied her with critical eyes and saw no change whatever.

One afternoon Billy Buck leaned the many-tined manure fork against the barn wall. He loosened his belt and tucked in his shirt-tail and tightened the belt again. He picked one of the little straws from his hatband and put it in the corner of his mouth. Jody, who was helping Doubletree Mutt, the big serious dog, to dig out a gopher, straightened up as the ranch hand sauntered out of the barn.

"Let's go up and have a look at Nellie," Billy suggested.

Instantly Jody fell into step with him. Doubletree Mutt watched them over his shoulder; then he dug furiously, growled, sounded little sharp yelps to indicate that the gopher was practically caught. When he looked over his shoulder again, and saw that neither Jody nor Billy was interested, he climbed reluctantly out of the hole and followed them up the hill.

The wild oats were ripening. Every head bent sharply under its load of grain, and the grass was dry enough so that it made a swishing sound as Jody and Billy stepped through it. Halfway up the hill they could see Nellie and the iron-grey gelding, Pete, nibbling the heads from the wild oats. When they approached, Nellie looked at them and backed her ears and bobbed her head up and down rebelliously. Billy walked to her and put his hand under her mane and patted her neck, until her ears came forward again and she nibbled delicately at his shirt.

Jody asked, "Do you think she's really going to have a colt?"

Billy rolled the lids back from the mare's eyes with his thumb and forefinger. He felt the lower lip and fingered the black, leathery teats. "I wouldn't be surprised," he said.

"Well, she isn't changed at all. It's three months gone."

Billy rubbed the mare's flat forehead with his knuckle while she grunted with pleasure. "I told you you'd get tired waiting. It'll be five months more before you can even see a sign, and it'll be at least eight months more before she throws the colt, about next January."

Jody sighed deeply. "It's a long time, isn't it?"

"And then it'll be about two years more before you can ride."

Jody cried out in despair, "I'll be grown up."

"Yep, you'll be an old man," said Billy.

"What color do you think the colt'll be?"

"Why, you can't ever tell. The stud is black and the dam is bay. Colt might be black or bay or grey or dappled. You can't tell. Sometimes a black dam might have a white colt."

"Well, I hope it's black, and a stallion."

"If it's a stallion, we'll have to geld it. Your father wouldn't let you have a stallion."

"Maybe he would," Jody said. "I could train him not to be mean."

Billy pursed his lips, and the little straw that had been in the corner of his mouth rolled down to the center. "You can't ever trust a stallion," he said critically. "They're mostly fighting and making trouble. Sometimes when they're feeling funny they won't work. They make the mares uneasy and kick hell out of the geldings. Your father wouldn't let you keep a stallion."

Nellie sauntered away, nibbling the drying grass. Jody skinned the grain from a grass stem and threw the handful into the air, so that each pointed, feathered seed sailed out like a dart. "Tell me how it'll be, Billy. Is it like when the cows have calves?"

"Just about. Mares are a little more sensitive. Sometimes you have to be there to help the mare. And sometimes if it's wrong, you have to——" he paused.

"Have to what, Billy?"

"Have to tear the colt to pieces to get it out, or the mare'll die."

"But it won't be that way this time, will it, Billy?"

"Oh, no. Nellie's thrown good colts."

"Can I be there, Billy? Will you be certain to call me? It's my colt."

"Sure, I'll call you. Of course I will."

"Tell me how it'll be."

"Why, you've seen the cows calving. It's almost the same. The mare starts groaning and stretching, and then, if it's a good right birth, the head and forefeet come out, and the front hoofs kick a hole just the way the calves do. And the colt starts to breathe. It's good to be there, 'cause if its feet aren't right maybe he can't break the sack, and then he might smother."

Jody whipped his leg with a bunch of grass. "We'll have to be there, then, won't we?"

"Oh, we'll be there, all right."

They turned and walked slowly down the hill toward the barn. Jody was tortured with a thing he had to say, although he didn't want to. "Billy," he began miserably, "Billy, you won't let anything happen to the colt, will you?"

And Billy knew he was thinking of the red pony, Gabilan, and of how it died of strangles. Billy knew he had been infallible before that, and now he was capable of failure. This knowledge made Billy much less sure of himself than he had been. "I can't tell," he said roughly. "All sorts of things might happen, and they wouldn't be my fault. I can't do everything." He felt badly about his lost prestige, and so he said meanly, "I'll do everything I know, but I won't promise anything. Nellie's a good mare. She's thrown good colts before. She ought to this time." And he walked away from Jody and went into the saddle-room beside the barn, for his feelings were hurt.

Jody traveled often to the brushline behind the house. A rusty iron pipe ran a thin stream of spring water into an old green tub. Where the water spilled over and sank into the ground there was a patch of perpetually green grass. Even when the hills were brown and baked in the summer that little patch was green. The water whined softly into the trough all the year round. This place had grown to be a center-point for Jody. When he had been punished the cool green grass and the singing water soothed him. When he had been mean the biting acid of meanness left him at the brushline. When he sat in the grass and listened to the purling stream, the barriers set up in his mind by the stern day went down to ruin.

On the other hand, the black cypress tree by the bunk-house was as repulsive as the water-tub was dear; for to this tree all the pigs came, sooner or later, to be slaughtered. Pig killing was fascinating, with the screaming and the blood, but it made Jody's heart beat so fast that it hurt him. After the pigs were scalded in the big iron tripod kettle and their skins were scraped and white, Jody had to go to the water-tub to sit in the grass until his heart grew quiet. The water-tub and the black cypress were opposites and enemies.

When Billy left him and walked angrily away, Jody turned up toward the house. He thought of Nellie as he walked, and of the little colt. Then suddenly he saw that he was under the black cypress, under the very singletree where the pigs were hung. He brushed his dry-grass hair off his forehead and hurried on. It seemed to him an unlucky thing to be thinking of his colt in the very slaughter place, especially after what Billy had said. To counteract any evil result of that bad conjunction he walked quickly past the ranch house, through the chicken yard, through the vegetable patch, until he came at last to the brushline.

He sat down in the green grass. The trilling water sounded in his ears. He looked over the farm buildings and across at the round hills, rich and yellow with grain. He could see Nellie feeding on the slope. As usual the water place eliminated time and distance. Jody saw a black, long-legged colt, butting against Nellie's flanks, demanding milk. And then he saw himself breaking a large colt to halter. All in a few moments the colt grew to be a magnificent animal, deep of chest, with a neck as high and arched as a sea-horse's neck, with a tail that tongued and rippled like black flame. This horse was terrible to everyone but Jody. In the schoolyard the boys begged rides, and Jody smilingly agreed. But no sooner were they mounted than the black demon pitched them off. Why, that was his name, Black Demon! For a moment the trilling water and the grass and the sunshine came back, and then . . .

Sometimes in the night the ranch people, safe in their beds, heard a roar of hoofs go by. They said, "It's Jody, on Demon. He's helping out the sheriff again." And then . . .

The golden dust filled the air in the arena at the Salinas Rodeo. The announcer called the roping contests. When Jody rode the black horse to the starting chute the other contestants shrugged and gave up first place, for it was well known that Jody and Demon could rope and throw and tie a steer a great deal quicker than any roping team of two men could. Jody was not a boy any more, and Demon was not a horse. The two together were one glorious individual. And then . . .

The President wrote a letter and asked them to help catch a bandit in Washington. Jody settled himself comfortably in the grass. The little stream of water whined into the mossy tub.

The year passed slowly on. Time after time Jody gave up his colt for lost. No change had taken place in Nellie. Carl Tiflin still drove her to a light cart, and she pulled on a hay rake and worked the Jackson-fork tackle when the hay was being put into the barn.

The summer passed, and the warm bright autumn. And then the frantic morning winds began to twist along the ground, and a chill came into the air, and the poison oak turned red. One morning in September, when he had finished his breakfast, Jody's mother called him into the kitchen. She was pouring boiling water into a bucket full of dry midlings and stirring the materials to a steaming paste.

"Yes, ma'am?" Jody asked.

"Watch how I do it. You'll have to do it after this every other morning."

"Well, what is it?"

"Why, it's warm mash for Nellie. It'll keep her in good shape."

Jody rubbed his forehead with a knuckle. "Is she all right?" he asked timidly.

Mrs. Tiflin put down the kettle and stirred the mash with a wooden paddle. "Of course she's all right, only you've got to take better care of her from now on. Here, take this breakfast out to her!"

Jody seized the bucket and ran, down past the bunk-house, past the barn, with the heavy bucket banging against his knees. He found Nellie playing with the water in the trough, pushing waves and tossing her head so that the water slopped out on the ground.

Jody climbed the fence and set the bucket of steaming mash beside her. Then he stepped back to look at her.

And she was changed. Her stomach was swollen. When she moved, her feet touched the ground gently. She buried her nose in the bucket and gobbled the hot breakfast. And when she had finished and had pushed the bucket around the ground with her nose a little, she stepped quietly over to Jody and rubbed her cheek against him.

Billy Buck came out of the saddle-room and walked over. "Starts fast when it starts, doesn't it?"

"Did it come all at once?"

"Oh, no, you just stopped looking for a while." He pulled her head around toward Jody. "She's goin' to be nice, too. See how nice her eyes are! Some mares get mean, but when they turn nice, they just love everything." Nellie slipped her head under Billy's arm and rubbed her neck up and down between his arm and his side. "You better treat her awful nice now," Billy said.

"How long will it be?" Jody demanded breathlessly.

The man counted in whispers on his fingers. "About three months," he said aloud. "You can't tell exactly. Sometimes it's eleven months to the day, but it might be two weeks early, or a month late, without hurting anything."

Jody looked hard at the ground. "Billy," he began nervously, "Billy, you'll call me when it's getting born, won't you? You'll let me be there, won't you?"

Billy bit the tip of Nellie's ear with his front teeth. "Carl says he wants you to start right at the start. That's the only way to learn. Nobody can tell you anything. Like my old man did with me about the saddle blanket. He was a government packer when I was your size, and I helped him some. One day I left a wrinkle in my saddle blanket and made a saddle-sore. My old man didn't give me hell at all. But the next morning he saddled me up with a forty-pound stock saddle. I had to lead my horse and carry that saddle over a whole damn mountain in the sun. It darn near killed me, but I never left no wrinkles in a blanket again. I couldn't. I never in my life since then put on a blanket but I felt that saddle on my back."

Jody reached up a hand and took hold of Nellie's mane. "You'll tell me what to do about everything, won't you? I guess you know everything about horses, don't you?"

Billy laughed. "Why I'm half horse myself, you see," he said. "My ma died when I was born, and being my old man was a government packer in the mountains, and no cows around most of the time, why he just gave me mostly mare's milk." He continued seriously, "And horses know that. Don't you know it, Nellie?"

The mare turned her head and looked full into his eyes for a moment, and this is a thing horses practically never do. Billy was proud and sure of himself now. He boasted a little. "I'll see you get a good colt. I'll start you right. And if you do like I say, you'll have the best horse in the county."

That made Jody feel warm and proud, too; so proud that when he went back to the house he bowed his legs and swayed his shoulders as horsemen do. And he whispered, "Whoa, you Black Demon, you! Steady down there and keep your feet on the ground."

The winter fell sharply. A few preliminary gusty showers, and then a strong steady rain. The hills lost their straw color and blackened under the water, and the winter streams scrambled noisily down the canyons. The mushrooms and puffballs popped up and the new grass started before Christmas.

But this year Christmas was not the central day to Jody. Some undetermined time in January had become the axis day around which the months swung. When the rains fell, he put Nellie in a box stall and fed her warm food every morning and curried her and brushed her.

The mare was swelling so greatly that Jody became alarmed. "She'll pop wide open," he said to Billy.

Billy laid his strong square hand against Nellie's swollen abdomen. "Feel here," he said quietly. "You can feel it move. I guess it would surprise you if there were twin colts."

"You don't think so?" Jody cried. "You don't think it will be twins, do you, Billy?"

"No, I don't, but it does happen, sometimes."

During the first two weeks of January it rained steadily. Jody spent most of his time, when he wasn't in school, in the box stall with Nellie. Twenty times a day he put his hand on her stomach to feel the colt move. Nellie became more and more gentle and friendly to him. She rubbed her nose on him. She whinnied softly when he walked into the barn.

Carl Tiflin came to the barn with Jody one day. He looked admiringly at the groomed bay coat, and he felt the firm flesh over ribs and shoulders. "You've done a good job," he said to Jody. And this was the greatest praise he knew how to give. Jody was tight with pride for hours afterward.

The fifteenth of January came, and the colt was not born. And the twentieth came; a lump of fear began to form in Jody's stomach. "Is it all right?" he demanded of Billy.

"Oh, sure."

And again, "Are you sure it's going to be all right?"

Billy stroked the mare's neck. She swayed her head uneasily. "I told you it wasn't always the same time, Jody. You just have to wait."

When the end of the month arrived with no birth,

Jody grew frantic. Nellie was so big that her breath came heavily, and her ears were close together and straight up, as though her head ached. Jody's sleep grew restless, and his dreams confused.

On the night of the second of February he awakened crying. His mother called to him, "Jody, you're dreaming. Wake up and start over again."

But Jody was filled with terror and desolation. He lay quietly a few moments, waiting for his mother to go back to sleep, and then he slipped his clothes on, and crept out in his bare feet.

The night was black and thick. A little misting rain fell. The cypress tree and the bunkhouse loomed and then dropped back into the mist. The barn door screeched as he opened it, a thing it never did in the daytime. Jody went to the rack and found a lantern and a tin box of matches. He lighted the wick and walked down the long straw-covered aisle to Nellie's stall. She was standing up. Her whole body weaved from side to side. Jody called to her, "So, Nellie, so-o, Nellie," but she did not stop her swaying nor look around. When he stepped into the stall and touched her on the shoulder she shivered under his hand. Then Billy Buck's voice came from the hayloft right above the stall.

"Jody, what are you doing?"

Jody started back and turned miserable eyes up toward the nest where Billy was lying in the hay. "Is she all right, do you think?"

"Why sure, I think so."

"You won't let anything happen, Billy, you're sure you won't?"

Billy growled down at him, "I told you I'd call you, and I will. Now you get back to bed and stop worrying that mare. She's got enough to do without you worrying her."

Jody cringed, for he had never heard Billy speak in such a tone. "I only thought I'd come and see," he said. "I woke up."

Billy softened a little then. "Well, you get to bed. I don't want you bothering her. I told you I'd get you a good colt. Get along now."

Jody walked slowly out of the barn. He blew out the lantern and set it in the rack. The blackness of the night, and the chilled mist struck him and enfolded him. He wished he believed everything Billy said as he had before the pony died. It was a moment before his eyes, blinded by the feeble lantern-flame, could make any form of the darkness. The damp ground chilled his bare feet. At the cypress tree the roosting turkeys chattered a little in alarm, and the two good dogs responded to their duty and came charging out, barking to frighten away the coyotes they thought were prowling under the tree.

As he crept through the kitchen, Jody stumbled over a chair. Carl called from his bedroom, "Who's there? What's the matter there?"

And Mrs. Tiflin said sleepily, "What's the matter, Carl?"

The next second Carl came out of the bedroom carrying a candle, and found Jody before he could get into bed. "What are you doing out?"

Jody turned shyly away. "I was down to see the mare."

For a moment anger at being awakened fought with approval in Jody's father. "Listen," he said, finally, "there's not a man in this country that knows more about colts than Billy. You leave it to him."

Words burst out of Jody's mouth. "But the pony died——"

"Don't you go blaming that on him," Carl said sternly. "If Billy can't save a horse, it can't be saved."

Mrs. Tiflin called, "Make him clean his feet and go to bed, Carl. He'll be sleepy all day tomorrow."

It seemed to Jody that he had just closed his eyes to try to go to sleep when he was shaken violently by the shoulder. Billy Buck stood beside him, holding a lantern in his hand. "Get up," he said. "Hurry up." He turned and walked quickly out of the room.

Mrs. Tiflin called, "What's the matter? Is that you, Billy?"

"Yes, ma'am."

"Is Nellie ready?"

"Yes, ma'am."

"All right, I'll get up and heat some water in case you need it."

Jody jumped into his clothes so quickly that he was out the back door before Billy's swinging lantern was halfway to the barn. There was a rim of dawn on the mountain-tops, but no light had penetrated into the cup of the ranch yet. Jody ran frantically after the lantern and caught up to Billy just as he reached the barn. Billy hung the lantern to a nail on the stall-side and took off his blue denim coat. Jody saw that he wore only a sleeveless shirt under it.

Nellie was standing rigid and stiff. While they watched, she crouched. Her whole body was wrung with a spasm. The spasm passed. But in a few moments it started over again, and passed.

Billy muttered nervously, "There's something wrong." His bare hand disappeared. "Oh, Jesus," he said. "It's wrong."

The spasm came again, and this time Billy strained, and the muscles stood out on his arm and shoulder. He heaved strongly, his forehead beaded with perspiration. Nellie cried with pain. Billy was muttering, "It's wrong.

I can't turn it. It's way wrong. It's turned all around wrong."

He glared wildly toward Jody. And then his fingers made a careful, careful diagnosis. His cheeks were growing tight and grey. He looked for a long questioning minute at Jody standing back of the stall. Then Billy stepped to the rack under the manure window and picked up a horseshoe hammer with his wet right hand.

"Go outside, Jody," he said.

The boy stood still and stared dully at him.

"Go outside, I tell you. It'll be too late."

Jody didn't move.

Then Billy walked quickly to Nellie's head. He cried, "Turn your face away, damn you, turn your face."

This time Jody obeyed. His head turned sideways. He heard Billy whispering hoarsely in the stall. And then he heard a hollow crunch of bone. Nellie chuckled shrilly. Jody looked back in time to see the hammer rise and fall again on the flat forehead. Then Nellie fell heavily to her side and quivered for a moment.

Billy jumped to the swollen stomach; his big pocket-knife was in his hand. He lifted the skin and drove the knife in. He sawed and ripped at the tough belly. The air filled with the sick odor of warm living entrails. The other horses reared back against their halter chains and squealed and kicked.

Billy dropped the knife. Both of his arms plunged into the terrible ragged hole and dragged out a big, white, dripping bundle. His teeth tore a hole in the covering. A little black head appeared through the tear, and little slick, wet ears. A gurgling breath was drawn, and then another. Billy shucked off the sac and found his knife and cut the string. For a moment he held the little black colt in his arms and looked at it. And then he walked slowly over and laid it in the straw at Jody's feet.

Billy's face and arms and chest were dripping red. His body shivered and his teeth chattered. His voice was gone; he spoke in a throaty whisper. "There's your colt. I promised. And there it is. I had to do it—had to." He stopped and looked over his shoulder into the box stall. "Go get hot water and a sponge," he whispered. "Wash him and dry him the way his mother would. You'll have to feed him by hand. But there's your colt, the way I promised."

Jody stared stupidly at the wet, panting foal. It stretched out its chin and tried to raise its head. Its blank eyes were navy blue.

"God damn you," Billy shouted, "will you go now for the water? *Will you go?*"

Then Jody turned and trotted out of the barn into the dawn. He ached from his throat to his stomach. His legs were stiff and heavy. He tried to be glad because of the colt, but the bloody face, and the haunted, tired eyes of Billy Buck hung in the air ahead of him.

IV. THE LEADER OF THE PEOPLE

ON SATURDAY afternoon Billy Buck, the ranch-hand, raked together the last of the old year's haystack and pitched small forkfuls over the wire fence to a few mildly interested cattle. High in the air small clouds like puffs of cannon smoke were driven eastward by the March wind. The wind could be heard whishing in the brush on the ridge crests, but no breath of it penetrated down into the ranch-cup.

The little boy, Jody, emerged from the house eating a thick piece of buttered bread. He saw Billy working on the last of the haystack. Jody tramped down scuffing his shoes in a way he had been told was destructive to good shoe-leather. A flock of white pigeons flew out of the black cypress tree as Jody passed, and circled the tree and landed again. A half-grown tortoise-shell cat leaped from the bunkhouse porch, galloped on stiff legs across the road, whirled and galloped back again. Jody picked up a stone to help the game along, but he was too late, for the cat was under the porch before the stone could be discharged. He threw the stone into the cypress tree and started the white pigeons on another whirling flight.

Arriving at the used-up haystack, the boy leaned against the barbed wire fence. "Will that be all of it, do you think?" he asked.

The middle-aged ranch-hand stopped his careful raking and stuck his fork into the ground. He took off his black hat and smoothed down his hair. "Nothing left of it that isn't soggy from ground moisture," he said. He replaced his hat and rubbed his dry leathery hands together.

"Ought to be plenty mice," Jody suggested.

"Lousy with them," said Billy. "Just crawling with mice."

"Well, maybe, when you get all through, I could call the dogs and hunt the mice."

"Sure, I guess you could," said Billy Buck. He lifted a forkful of the damp ground-hay and threw it into the air. Instantly three mice leaped out and burrowed frantically under the hay again.

Jody sighed with satisfaction. Those plump, sleek, arrogant mice were doomed. For eight months they had lived and multiplied in the haystack. They had been immune from cats, from traps, from poison and from Jody. They had grown smug in their security, overbearing and fat. Now the time of disaster had come; they would not survive another day.

Billy looked up at the top of the hills that surrounded the ranch. "Maybe you better ask your father before you do it," he suggested.

"Well, where is he? I'll ask him now."

"He rode up to the ridge ranch after dinner. He'll be back pretty soon."

Jody slumped against the fence post. "I don't think he'd care."

As Billy went back to his work he said ominously, "You'd better ask him anyway. You know how he is."

Jody did know. His father, Carl Tiflin, insisted upon giving permission for anything that was done on the ranch, whether it was important or not. Jody sagged farther against the post until he was sitting on the ground. He looked up at the little puffs of wind-driven cloud. "Is it like to rain, Billy?"

"It might. The wind's good for it, but not strong enough."

"Well, I hope it don't rain until after I kill those damn mice." He looked over his shoulder to see whether Billy had noticed the mature profanity. Billy worked on without comment.

Jody turned back and looked at the side-hill where the road from the outside world came down. The hill was washed with lean March sunshine. Silver thistles, blue lupins and a few poppies bloomed among the sage bushes. Halfway up the hill Jody could see Doubletree Mutt, the black dog, digging in a squirrel hole. He paddled for a while and then paused to kick bursts of dirt out between his hind legs, and he dug with an earnestness which belied the knowledge he must have had that no dog had ever caught a squirrel by digging in a hole.

Suddenly, while Jody watched, the black dog stiffened, and backed out of the hole and looked up the hill toward the cleft in the ridge where the road came through. Jody looked up too. For a moment Carl Tiflin on horseback stood out against the pale sky and then he moved down the road toward the house. He carried something white in his hand.

The boy started to his feet. "He's got a letter," Jody cried. He trotted away toward the ranch house, for the letter would probably be read aloud and he wanted to be there. He reached the house before his father did, and ran in. He heard Carl dismount from his creaking saddle and slap the horse on the side to send it to the barn where Billy would unsaddle it and turn it out.

Jody ran into the kitchen. "We got a letter!" he cried.

His mother looked up from a pan of beans. "Who has?"

"Father has. I saw it in his hand."

Carl strode into the kitchen then, and Jody's mother asked, "Who's the letter from, Carl?"

He frowned quickly. "How did you know there was a letter?"

She nodded her head in the boy's direction. "Big-Britches Jody told me."

Jody was embarrassed.

His father looked down at him contemptuously. "He *is* getting to be a Big-Britches," Carl said. "He's minding everybody's business but his own. Got his big nose into everything."

Mrs. Tiflin relented a little. "Well, he hasn't enough to keep him busy. Who's the letter from?"

Carl still frowned on Jody. "I'll keep him busy if he isn't careful." He held out a sealed letter. "I guess it's from your father."

Mrs. Tiflin took a hairpin from her head and slit open the flap. Her lips pursed judiciously. Jody saw her eyes snap back and forth over the lines. "He says," she translated, "he says he's going to drive out Saturday to stay for a little while. Why, this is Saturday. The letter must have been delayed." She looked at the postmark. "This was mailed day before yesterday. It should have been here yesterday." She looked up questioningly at her husband, and then her face darkened angrily. "Now what have you got that look on you for? He doesn't come often."

Carl turned his eyes away from her anger. He could be stern with her most of the time, but when occasionally her temper arose, he could not combat it.

"What's the matter with you?" she demanded again.

In his explanation there was a tone of apology Jody himself might have used. "It's just that he talks," Carl said lamely. "Just talks."

"Well, what of it? You talk yourself."

"Sure I do. But your father only talks about one thing."

"Indians!" Jody broke in excitedly. "Indians and crossing the plains!"

Carl turned fiercely on him. "You get out, Mr. Big-Britches! Go on, now! Get out!"

Jody went miserably out the back door and closed the screen with elaborate quietness. Under the kitchen window his shamed, downcast eyes fell upon a curiously shaped stone, a stone of such fascination that he squatted down and picked it up and turned it over in his hands.

The voices came clearly to him through the open kitchen window. "Jody's damn well right," he heard his father say. "Just Indians and crossing the plains. I've heard that story about how the horses got driven off about a thousand times. He just goes on and on, and he never changes a word in the things he tells."

When Mrs. Tiflin answered her tone was so changed that Jody, outside the window, looked up from his study of the stone. Her voice had become soft and explanatory.

Jody knew how her face would have changed to match the tone. She said quietly, "Look at it this way, Carl. That was the big thing in my father's life. He led a wagon train clear across the plains to the coast,, and when it was finished, his life was done. It was a big thing to do, but it didn't last long enough. Look!" she continued, "it's as though he was born to do that, and after he finished it, there wasn't anything more for him to do but think about it and talk about it. If there'd been any farther west to go, he'd have gone. He's told me so himself. But at last there was the ocean. He lives right by the ocean where he had to stop."

She had caught Carl, caught him and entangled him in her soft tone.

"I've seen him," he agreed quietly. "He goes down and stares off west over the ocean." His voice sharpened a little. "And then he goes up to the Horseshoe Club in Pacific Grove, and he tells people how the Indians drove off the horses."

She tried to catch him again. "Well, it's everything to him. You might be patient with him and pretend to listen."

Carl turned impatiently away. "Well, if it gets too bad, I can always go down to the bunkhouse and sit with Billy," he said irritably. He walked through the house and slammed the front door after him.

Jody ran to his chores. He dumped the grain to the chickens without chasing any of them. He gathered the eggs from the nests. He trotted into the house with the wood and interlaced it so carefully in the wood-box that two armloads seemed to fill it to overflowing.

His mother had finished the beans by now. She stirred up the fire and brushed off the stove-top with a turkey wing. Jody peered cautiously at her to see whether any rancor toward him remained. "Is he coming today?" Jody asked.

"That's what his letter said."

"Maybe I better walk up the road to meet him."

Mrs. Tiflin clanged the stove-lid shut. "That would be nice," she said. "He'd probably like to be met."

"I guess I'll just do it then."

Outside, Jody whistled shrilly to the dogs. "Come on up the hill," he commanded. The two dogs waved their tails and ran ahead. Along the roadside the sage had tender new tips. Jody tore off some pieces and rubbed them on his hands until the air was filled with the sharp wild smell. With a rush the dogs leaped from the road and yapped into the brush after a rabbit. That was the last Jody saw of them, for when they failed to catch the rabbit, they went back home.

Jody plodded on up the hill toward the ridge top. When he reached the little cleft where the road came through, the afternoon wind struck him and blew up his hair and ruffled his shirt. He looked down on the little hills and ridges below and then out at the huge green Salinas Valley. He could see the white town of Salinas far out in the flat and the flash of its windows under the waning sun. Directly below him, in an oak tree, a crow congress had convened. The tree was black with crows all cawing at once.

Then Jody's eyes followed the wagon road down from the ridge where he stood, and lost it behind a hill, and picked it up again on the other side. On that distant stretch he saw a cart slowly pulled by a bay horse. It disappeared behind the hill. Jody sat down on the ground and watched the place where the cart would reappear again. The wind sang on the hilltops and the puff-ball clouds hurried eastward.

Then the cart came into sight and stopped. A man

dressed in black dismounted from the seat and walked to the horse's head. Although it was so far away, Jody knew he had unhooked the check-rein, for the horse's head dropped forward. The horse moved on, and the man walked slowly up the hill beside it. Jody gave a glad cry and ran down the road toward them. The squirrels bumped along off the road, and a road-runner flirted its tail and raced over the edge of the hill and sailed out like a glider.

Jody tried to leap into the middle of his shadow at every step. A stone rolled under his foot and he went down. Around a little bend he raced, and there, a short distance ahead, were his grandfather and the cart. The boy dropped from his unseemly running and approached at a dignified walk.

The horse plodded stumble-footedly up the hill and the old man walked beside it. In the lowering sun their giant shadows flickered darkly behind them. The grandfather was dressed in a black broadcloth suit and he wore kid congress gaiters and a black tie on a short, hard collar. He carried his black slouch hat in his hand. His white beard was cropped close and his white eyebrows overhung his eyes like mustaches. The blue eyes were sternly merry. About the whole face and figure there was a granite dignity, so that every motion seemed an impossible thing. Once at rest, it seemed the old man would be stone, would never move again. His steps were slow and certain. Once made, no step could ever be retraced; once headed in a direction, the path would never bend nor the pace increase nor slow.

When Jody appeared around the bend, Grandfather waved his hat slowly in welcome, and he called, "Why, Jody! Come down to meet me, have you?"

Jody sidled near and turned and matched his step to the old man's step and stiffened his body and dragged his heels a little. "Yes, sir," he said. "We got your letter only today."

"Should have been here yesterday," said Grandfather. "It certainly should. How are all the folks?"

"They're fine, sir." He hesitated and then suggested shyly. "Would you like to come on a mouse hunt tomorrow, sir?"

"Mouse hunt, Jody?" Grandfather chuckled. "Have the people of this generation come down to hunting mice? They aren't very strong, the new people, but I hardly thought mice would be game for them."

"No, sir. It's just play. The haystack's gone. I'm going to drive out the mice to the dogs. And you can watch, or even beat the hay a little."

The stern, merry eyes turned down on him. "I see. You don't eat them, then. You haven't come to that yet."

Jody explained, "The dogs eat them, sir. It wouldn't be much like hunting Indians, I guess."

"No, not much—but then later, when the troops were hunting Indians and shooting children and burning tee-pees, it wasn't much different from your mouse hunt."

They topped the rise and started down into the ranch cup, and they lost the sun from their shoulders. "You've grown," Grandfather said. "Nearly an inch, I should say."

"More," Jody boasted. "Where they mark me on the door, I'm up more than an inch since Thanksgiving even."

Grandfather's rich throaty voice said, "Maybe you're getting too much water and turning to pith and stalk. Wait until you head out, and then we'll see."

Jody looked quickly into the old man's face to see whether his feelings should be hurt, but there was no will to injure, no punishing nor putting-in-your-place light in the keen blue eyes. "We might kill a pig," Jody suggested.

"Oh, no! I couldn't let you do that. You're just humoring me. It isn't the time and you know it."

"You know Riley, the big boar, sir?"

"Yes, I remember Riley well."

"Well, Riley ate a hole into that same haystack, and it fell down on him and smothered him."

"Pigs do that when they can," said Grandfather.

"Riley was a nice pig, for a boar, sir. I rode him sometimes, and he didn't mind."

A door slammed at the house below them, and they saw Jody's mother standing on the porch waving her apron in welcome. And they saw Carl Tiflin walking up from the barn to be at the house for the arrival.

The sun had disappeared from the hills by now. The blue smoke from the house chimney hung in flat layers in the purpling ranch-cup. The puff-ball clouds, dropped by the falling wind, hung listlessly in the sky.

Billy Buck came out of the bunkhouse and flung a wash basin of soapy water on the ground. He had been shaving in mid-week, for Billy held Grandfather in reverence, and Grandfather said that Billy was one of the few men of the new generation who had not gone soft. Although Billy was in middle age, Grandfather considered him a boy. Now Billy was hurrying toward the house too.

When Jody and Grandfather arrived, the three were waiting for them in front of the yard gate.

Carl said, "Hello, sir. We've been looking for you."

Mrs. Tiflin kissed Grandfather on the side of his beard, and stood still while his big hand patted her shoulder. Billy shook hands solemnly, grinning under his straw mustache. "I'll put up your horse," said Billy, and he led the rig away.

The Red Pony

Grandfather watched him go, and then, turning back to the group, he said as he had said a hundred times before, "There's a good boy. I knew his father, old Mule-tail Buck. I never knew why they called him Mule-tail except he packed mules."

Mrs. Tiflin turned and led the way into the house. "How long are you going to stay, Father? Your letter didn't say."

"Well, I don't know. I thought I'd stay about two weeks. But I never stay as long as I think I'm going to."

In a short while they were sitting at the white oilcloth table eating their supper. The lamp with the tin reflector hung over the table. Outside the dining-room windows the big moths battered softly against the glass.

Grandfather cut his steak into tiny pieces and chewed slowly. "I'm hungry," he said. "Driving out here got my appetite up. It's like when we were crossing. We all got so hungry every night we could hardly wait to let the meat get done. I could eat about five pounds of buffalo meat every night."

"It's moving around does it," said Billy. "My father was a government packer. I helped him when I was a kid. Just the two of us could about clean up a deer's ham."

"I knew your father, Billy," said Grandfather. "A fine man he was. They called him Mule-tail Buck. I don't know why except he packed mules."

"That was it," Billy agreed. "He packed mules."

Grandfather put down his knife and fork and looked around the table. "I remember one time we ran out of meat—" His voice dropped to a curious low sing-song, dropped into a tonal groove the story had worn for itself. "There was no buffalo, no antelope, not even rabbits. The hunters couldn't even shoot a coyote. That was the time for the leader to be on the watch. I was the leader, and I kept my eyes open. Know why? Well, just the minute the people began to get hungry they'd start slaughtering the team oxen. Do you believe that? I've heard of parties that just ate up their draft cattle. Started from the middle and worked toward the ends. Finally they'd eat the lead pair, and then the wheelers. The leader of a party had to keep them from doing that."

In some manner a big moth got into the room and circled the hanging kerosene lamp. Billy got up and tried to clap it between his hands. Carl struck with a cupped palm and caught the moth and broke it. He walked to the window and dropped it out.

"As I was saying," Grandfather began again, but Carl interrupted him. "You'd better eat some more meat. All the rest of us are ready for our pudding."

Jody saw a flash of anger in his mother's eyes. Grandfather picked up his knife and fork. "I'm pretty hungry, all right," he said. "I'll tell you about that later."

When supper was over, when the family and Billy Buck sat in front of the fireplace in the other room, Jody anxiously watched Grandfather. He saw the signs he knew. The bearded head leaned forward; the eyes lost their sternness and looked wonderingly into the fire; the big lean fingers laced themselves on the black knees. "I wonder," he began, "I just wonder whether I ever told you how those thieving Piutes drove off thirty-five of our horses."

"I think you did," Carl interrupted. "Wasn't it just before you went up into the Tahoe country?"

Grandfather turned quickly toward his son-in-law. "That's right. I guess I must have told you that story."

"Lots of times," Carl said cruelly, and he avoided his wife's eyes. But he felt the angry eyes on him, and he said, "Course I'd like to hear it again."

Grandfather looked back at the fire. His fingers un-

The Red Pony

laced and laced again. Jody knew how he felt, how his insides were collapsed and empty. Hadn't Jody been called a Big-Britches that very afternoon? He arose to heroism and opened himself to the term Big-Britches again. "Tell about Indians," he said softly.

Grandfather's eyes grew stern again. "Boys always want to hear about Indians. It was a job for men, but boys want to hear about it. Well, let's see. Did I ever tell you how I wanted each wagon to carry a long iron plate?"

Everyone but Jody remained silent. Jody said, "No. You didn't."

"Well, when the Indians attacked, we always put the wagons in a circle and fought from between the wheels. I thought that if every wagon carried a long plate with rifle holes, the men could stand the plates on the outside of the wheels when the wagons were in the circle and they would be protected. It would save lives and that would make up for the extra weight of the iron. But of course the party wouldn't do it. No party had done it before and they couldn't see why they should go to the expense. They lived to regret it, too."

Jody looked at his mother, and knew from her expression that she was not listening at all. Carl picked at a callus on his thumb and Billy Buck watched a spider crawling up the wall.

Grandfather's tone dropped into its narrative groove again. Jody knew in advance exactly what words would fall. The story droned on, speeded up for the attack, grew sad over the wounds, struck a dirge at the burials on the great plains. Jody sat quietly watching Grandfather. The stern blue eyes were detached. He looked as though he were not very interested in the story himself.

When it was finished, when the pause had been politely respected as the frontier of the story, Billy Buck stood up and stretched and hitched his trousers. "I guess

I'll turn in," he said. Then he faced Grandfather. "I've got an old powder horn and a cap and ball pistol down to the bunkhouse. Did I ever show them to you?"

Grandfather nodded slowly. "Yes, I think you did, Billy. Reminds me of a pistol I had when I was leading the people across." Billy stood politely until the little story was done, and then he said, "Good night," and went out of the house.

Carl Tiflin tried to turn the conversation then. "How's the country between here and Monterey? I've heard it's pretty dry."

"It is dry," said Grandfather. "There's not a drop of water in the Laguna Seca. But it's a long pull from '87. The whole country was powder then, and in '61 I believe all the coyotes starved to death. We had fifteen inches of rain this year."

"Yes, but it all came too early. We could do with some now." Carl's eyes fell on Jody. "Hadn't you better be getting to bed?"

Jody stood up obediently. "Can I kill the mice in the old haystack, sir?"

"Mice? Oh! Sure, kill them all off. Billy said there isn't any good hay left."

Jody exchanged a secret and satisfying look with Grandfather. "I'll kill every one tomorrow," he promised.

Jody lay in his bed and thought of the impossible world of Indians and buffaloes, a world that had ceased to be forever. He wished he could have been living in the heroic time, but he knew he was not of heroic timber. No one living now, save possibly Billy Buck, was worthy to do the things that had been done. A race of giants had lived then, fearless men, men of a staunchness unknown in this day. Jody thought of the wide plains and of the wagons moving across like centipedes. He thought of Grandfather on a huge white horse, marshaling the people. Across his mind marched the great phantoms, and they marched off the earth and they were gone.

He came back to the ranch for a moment, then. He heard the dull rushing sound that space and silence make. He heard one of the dogs, out in the doghouse, scratching a flea and bumping his elbow against the floor with every stroke. Then the wind arose again and the black cypress groaned and Jody went to sleep.

He was up half an hour before the triangle sounded for breakfast. His mother was rattling the stove to make the flames roar when Jody went through the kitchen. "You're up early," she said. "Where are you going?"

"Out to get a good stick. We're going to kill the mice today."

"Who is 'we'?"

"Why, Grandfather and I."

"So you've got him in it. You always like to have someone in with you in case there's blame to share."

"I'll be right back," said Jody. "I just want to have a good stick ready for after breakfast."

He closed the screen door after him and went out into the cool blue morning. The birds were noisy in the dawn and the ranch cats came down from the hill like blunt snakes. They had been hunting gophers in the dark, and although the four cats were full of gopher meat, they sat in a semi-circle at the back door and mewed piteously for milk. Doubletree Mutt and Smasher moved sniffing along the edge of the brush, performing the duty with rigid ceremony, but when Jody whistled, their heads jerked up and their tails waved. They plunged down to him, wriggling their skins and yawning. Jody patted their heads seriously, and moved on to the weathered scrap pile. He selected an old broom handle and a short piece of inch-square scrap wood. From his pocket he took a shoelace and tied the ends of the sticks loosely together to make a flail. He whistled his new weapon through the air and struck the ground experimentally, while the dogs leaped aside and whined with apprehension.

Jody turned and started down past the house toward the old haystack ground to look over the field of slaughter, but Billy Buck, sitting patiently on the back steps, called to him, "You better come back. It's only a couple of minutes till breakfast."

Jody changed his course and moved toward the house. He leaned his flail against the steps. "That's to drive the mice out," he said. "I'll bet they're fat, I'll bet they don't know what's going to happen to them today."

"No, nor you either," Billy remarked philosophically, "nor me, nor anyone."

Jody was staggered by this thought. He knew it was true. His imagination twitched away from the mouse hunt. Then his mother came out on the back porch and struck the triangle, and all thoughts fell in a heap.

Grandfather hadn't appeared at the table when they sat down. Billy nodded at his empty chair. "He's all right? He isn't sick?"

"He takes a long time to dress," said Mrs. Tiflin. "He combs his whiskers and rubs up his shoes and brushes his clothes."

Carl scattered sugar on his mush. "A man that's led a wagon train across the plains has got to be pretty careful how he dresses."

Mrs. Tiflin turned on him. "Don't do that, Carl! Please don't!" There was more of threat than of request in her tone. And the threat irritated Carl.

"Well, how many times do I have to listen to the story of the iron plates, and the thirty-five horses? That time's done. Why can't he forget it, now it's done?" He grew angrier while he talked and his voice rose. "Why does he have to tell them over and over? He came across the plains. All right! Now it's finished. Nobody wants to hear about it over and over."

The door into the kitchen closed softly. The four at the table sat frozen. Carl laid his mush spoon on the table and touched his chin with his fingers.

Then the kitchen door opened and Grandfather walked in. His mouth smiled tightly and his eyes were squinted. "Good morning," he said, and he sat down and looked at his mush dish.

Carl could not leave it there. "Did—did you hear what I said?"

Grandfather jerked a little nod.

"I don't know what got into me, sir. I didn't mean it. I was just being funny."

Jody glanced in shame at his mother, and he saw that she was looking at Carl, and that she wasn't breathing. It was an awful thing that he was doing. He was tearing himself to pieces to talk like that. It was a terrible thing to him to retract a word, but to retract it in shame was infinitely worse.

Grandfather looked sidewise. "I'm trying to get right side up," he said gently. "I'm not being mad. I don't mind what you said, but it might be true, and I would mind that."

"It isn't true," said Carl. "I'm not feeling well this morning. I'm sorry I said it."

"Don't be sorry, Carl. An old man doesn't see things sometimes. Maybe you're right. The crossing is finished. Maybe it should be forgotten, now it's done."

Carl got up from the table. "I've had enough to eat. I'm going to work. Take your time, Billy!" He walked quickly out of the dining-room. Billy gulped the rest of his food and followed soon after. But Jody could not leave his chair.

"Won't you tell any more stories?" Jody asked.

"Why, sure I'll tell them, but only when—I'm sure people want to hear them."

"I like to hear them, sir."

"Oh! Of course you do, but you're a little boy. It was a job for men, but only little boys like to hear about it."

Jody got up from his place. "I'll wait outside for you, sir. I've got a good stick for those mice."

He waited by the gate until the old man came out on the porch. "Let's go down and kill the mice now," Jody called.

"I think I'll just sit in the sun, Jody. You go kill the mice."

"You can use my stick if you like."

"No, I'll just sit here a while."

Jody turned disconsolately away, and walked down toward the old haystack. He tried to whip up his enthusiasm with thoughts of the fat juicy mice. He beat the ground with his flail. The dogs coaxed and whined about him, but he could not go. Back at the house he could see Grandfather sitting on the porch, looking small and thin and black.

Jody gave up and went to sit on the steps at the old man's feet.

"Back already? Did you kill the mice?"

"No, sir. I'll kill them some other day."

The morning flies buzzed close to the ground and the ants dashed about in front of the steps. The heavy smell of sage slipped down the hill. The porch boards grew warm in the sunshine.

Jody hardly knew when Grandfather started to talk. "I shouldn't stay here, feeling the way I do." He examined his strong old hands. "I feel as though the crossing wasn't worth doing." His eyes moved up the side-hill and stopped on a motionless hawk perched on a dead limb. "I tell those old stories, but they're not what I want to tell. I only know how I want people to feel when I tell them.

"It wasn't Indians that were important, nor adventures, nor even getting out here. It was a whole bunch of people made into one big crawling beast. And I was the head. It was westering and westering. Every man wanted something for himself, but the big beast that was all of them wanted only westering. I was the leader, but if I hadn't been there, someone else would have been the head. The thing had to have a head.

"Under the little bushes the shadows were black at white noonday. When we saw the mountains at last, we cried—all of us. But it wasn't getting here that mattered, it was movement and westering.

"We carried life out here and set it down the way those ants carry eggs. And I was the leader. The westering was as big as God, and the slow steps that made the movement piled up and piled up until the continent was crossed.

"Then we came down to the sea, and it was done." He stopped and wiped his eyes until the rims were red. "That's what I should be telling instead of stories."

When Jody spoke, Grandfather started and looked down at him. "Maybe I could lead the people some day," Jody said.

The old man smiled. "There's no place to go. There's the ocean to stop you. There's a line of old men along the shore hating the ocean because it stopped them."

"In boats I might, sir."

"No place to go, Jody. Every place is taken. But that's not the worst—no, not the worst. Westering has died out of the people. Westering isn't a hunger any more. It's all done. Your father is right. It is finished." He laced his fingers on his knee and looked at them.

Jody felt very sad. "If you'd like a glass of lemonade I could make it for you."

Grandfather was about to refuse, and then he saw Jody's face. "That would be nice," he said. "Yes, it would be nice to drink a lemonade."

Jody ran into the kitchen where his mother was wiping the last of the breakfast dishes. "Can I have a lemon to make a lemonade for Grandfather?"

His mother mimicked— "And another lemon to make a lemonade for you."

"No, ma'am. I don't want one."

"Jody! You're sick!" Then she stopped suddenly. "Take a lemon out of the cooler," she said softly. "Here, I'll reach the squeezer down to you."

JUNIUS MALTBY

JUNIUS MALTBY

JUNIUS MALTBY was a small young man of good and cultured family and decent education. When his father died bankrupt, Junius got himself inextricably entangled in a clerkship, against which he feebly struggled for ten years.

After work Junius retired to his furnished room, patted the cushions of his morris chair and spent the evening reading. Stevenson's essays he thought nearly the finest things in English: he read *Travels with a Donkey* many times.

One evening soon after his thirty-fifth birthday, Junius fainted on the steps of his boarding house. When he recovered consciousness, he noticed for the first time that his breathing was difficult and unsatisfactory. He wondered how long it had been that way. The doctor whom he consulted was kind and even hopeful.

"You're by no means too far gone to get well," he said. "But you really must take those lungs out of San Francisco. If you stay here in the fog, you won't live a year. Move to a warm, dry climate."

The accident to his health filled Junius with pleasure, for it cut the strings he had been unable to sever for himself. He had five hundred dollars, not that he ever saved any money; he had simply forgotten to spend it. "With that much," he said, "I'll either recover and make a clean, new start, or else I'll die and be through with the whole business."

A man in his office told him of the warm, protected

valley, the Pastures of Heaven, and Junius went there immediately. The name pleased him. "It's either an omen that I'm not going to live," he thought, "or else it's a nice symbolic substitute for death." He felt that the name meant something personal to him, and he was very glad, because for ten years nothing in the world had been personal to him.

There were, in the Pastures of Heaven, several families who wanted to take boarders. Junius inspected each one, and finally went to live on the farm of the widow Quaker. She needed the money, and besides, he could sleep in a shed separated from the farmhouse. Mrs. Quaker had two small boys and kept a hired man to work the farm.

The warm climate worked tenderly with Junius' lungs. Within the year his colour was good and he had gained in weight. He was quiet and happy on the farm, and what pleased him more, he had thrown out the ten years of the office and had grown superbly lazy. Junius' thin blond hair went uncombed; he wore his glasses far down on his square nose, for his eyes were getting stronger and only the habit of feeling spectacles caused him to wear them. Throughout the day he had always some small stick protruding from his mouth, a habit only the laziest and most ruminative of men acquire. This convalescence took place in 1910.

In 1911, Mrs. Quaker began to worry about what the neighbours were saying. When she considered the implication of having a single man in her house, she became upset and nervous. As soon as Junius' recovery seemed sure beyond doubt, the widow confessed her trepidations. He married her, immediately and gladly. Now he had a home and a golden future, for the new Mrs. Maltby owned two hundred acres of grassy hillside and five acres of orchard and vegetable bottom. Junius sent for his books, his morris chair with the adjustable back, and his good copy of Velasquez' *Cardinal*. The future was a pleasant and sunshiny afternoon to him.

Mrs. Maltby promptly discharged the hired man and tried to put her husband to work; but in this she encountered a resistance the more bewildering because it presented no hard front to strike at. During his convalescence, Junius had grown to love laziness. He liked the valley and the farm, but he liked them as they were: he didn't want to plant new things, nor to tear out old. When Mrs. Maltby put a hoe in his hand and set him to work in the vegetable garden, she found him, likely enough, hours later, dangling his feet in the meadow stream and reading his pocket copy of *Kidnapped*. He was sorry; he didn't know how it had happened. And that was the truth.

At first she nagged him a great deal about his laziness and his sloppiness of dress, but he soon developed a faculty for never listening to her. It would be impolite, he considered, to notice her when she was not being a lady. It would be like staring at a cripple. And Mrs. Maltby, after she had battered at his resistance of fog for a time, took to sniveling and neglecting her hair.

Between 1911, and 1917, the Maltbys grew very poor. Junius simply would not take care of the farm. They even sold a few acres of pasture land to get money for food and clothing, and even then there was never enough to eat. Poverty sat cross-legged on the farm, and the Maltbys were ragged. They had never any new clothes at all, but Junius had discovered the essays of David Grayson. He wore overalls and sat under the sycamores that lined the meadow stream. Sometimes he read *Adventures in Contentment* to his wife and two sons.

Early in 1917, Mrs. Maltby found that she was going to have a baby, and late in the same year the wartime influenza epidemic struck the family with a dry viciousness. Perhaps because they were undernourished the two boys were stricken simultaneously. For three days the house seemed filled to overflowing with flushed, feverish children whose nervous fingers strove to cling to life by the threads of their bed clothes. For three days they struggled weakly, and on the fourth, both of the boys died. Their mother didn't know it, for she was confined, and the neighbours who came to help in the house hadn't the courage nor the cruelty to tell her. The black fever came upon her while she was in labour and killed her before she ever saw her child.

The neighbour women who helped at the birth told the story throughout the valley that Junius Maltby read books by the stream while his wife and children died. But this was only partly true. On the day of their seizure, he dangled his feet in the stream, because he didn't know they were ill, but thereafter he wandered vaguely from one to the other of the dying children, and talked nonsense to them. He told the eldest boy how diamonds are made. At the bedside of the other, he explained the beauty, the antiquity and the symbolism of the swastika. One life went out while he read aloud the second chapter of *Treasure Island,* and he didn't even know it had happened until he finished the chapter and looked up. During those days he was bewildered. He brought out the only things he had and offered them, but they had not potency with death. He knew in advance they wouldn't have, and that made it all the more terrible to him.

When the bodies were all gone, Junius went back to the stream and read a few pages of *Travels with a Donkey*. He chuckled uncertainly over the obstinacy of Modestine. Who but Stevenson could have named a donkey "Modestine"?

One of the neighbour women called him in and cursed him so violently that he was embarrassed and didn't listen. She put her hands on her hips and glared at him with contempt. And then she brought his child, a son, and laid it in his arms. When she looked back at him from the gate, he was standing with the howling little brute in his arms. He couldn't see any place to put it down, so he held it for a long time.

The people of the valley told many stories about Junius. Sometimes they hated him with the loathing busy people have for lazy ones, and sometimes they envied his laziness; but often they pitied him because he blundered so. No one in the valley ever realized that he was happy.

They told how, on a doctor's advice, Junius bought a goat to milk for the baby. He didn't inquire into the sex of his purchase nor give his reason for wanting a goat. When it arrived he looked under it, and very seriously asked, "Is this a normal goat?"

"Sure," said the owner.

"But shouldn't there be a bag or something immediately behind the hind legs?—for the milk, I mean."

The people of the valley roared about that. Later, when a new and better goat was provided, Junius fiddled with it for two days and could not draw a drop of milk. He wanted to return this goat as defective until the owner showed him how to milk it. Some people claimed that he held the baby under the goat and let it suck its own milk, but this was untrue. The people of the valley declared they didn't know how he ever reared the child.

One day Junius went into Monterey and hired an old German to help him on the farm. He gave his new servant five dollars on account, and never paid him again. Within two weeks the hired man was so entangled in laziness that he did no more work than his employer. The two of them sat around the place together discussing things which interested and puzzled them—how colour comes to flowers—whether there is a symbology in nature —where Atlantis lay—how the Incas interred their dead.

In the spring they planted potatoes, always too late, and without a covering of ashes to keep the bugs out. They sowed beans and corn and peas, watched them for a time, and then forgot them. The weeds covered everything from sight. It was no unusual thing to see Junius burrow into a perfect thicket of mallow weeds and emerge carrying a pale cucumber. He had stopped wearing shoes because he liked the feeling of the warm earth on his feet, and because he had no shoes.

In the afternoon Junius talked to Jakob Stutz a great deal. "You know," he said, "when the children died, I thought I had reached a peculiar high peak of horror. Then, almost while I thought it, the horror turned to sorrow and the sorrow dwindled to sadness. I didn't know my wife nor the children very well, I guess. Perhaps they were too near to me. It's a strange thing, this *knowing*. It is nothing but an awareness of details. There are long visioned minds and short visioned. I've never been able to see things that are close to me. For instance, I am much more aware of the Parthenon than of my own house over there." Suddenly Junius' face seemed to quiver with feeling, and his eyes brightened with enthusiasm. "Jakob," he said, "have you ever seen a picture of the frieze of the Parthenon?"

"Yes, and it is good, too," said Jakob.

Junius laid a hand on his hired man's knee. "Those horses," he said. "Those lovely horses—bound for a celestial pasture. Those eager and yet dignified young men setting out for an incredible fiesta that's being celebrated just around the cornice. I wonder how a man can know what a horse feels like when it is very happy;

and that sculptor must have known or he couldn't have carved them so."

That was the way it went. Junius could not stay on a subject. Often the men went hungry because they failed to find a hen's nest in the grass when it came suppertime.

The son of Junius was named Robert Louis. Junius called him that when he thought of it, but Jakob Stutz rebelled at what he considered a kind of literary preciousness. "Boys must be named like dogs," he maintained. "One sound is sufficient for the name. Even Robert is too long. He should be called 'Bob.'" Jakob nearly got his way.

"I'll compromise with you," said Junius. "We'll call him Robbie. Robbie is really shorter than Robert, don't you think?"

He often gave way before Jakob, for Jakob continually struggled a little against the webs that were being spun about him. Now and then, with a kind of virtuous fury, he cleaned the house.

Robbie grew up gravely. He followed the men about, listening to their discussions. Junius never treated him like a little boy, because he didn't know how little boys should be treated. If Robbie made an observation the two men listened courteously and included the remark in their conversation, or even used it as the germ of an investigation. They tracked down many things in the course of an afternoon. Every day there were several raids on Junius' Encyclopedia.

A huge sycamore put out a horizontal limb over the meadow stream, and on it the three sat, the man hanging their feet into the water and moving pebbles with their toes while Robbie tried extravagantly to imitate them. Reaching the water was one of his criteria of manhood. Jakob had by this time given up shoes; Robbie had never worn any in his life.

The discussions were erudite. Robbie couldn't use childish talk, for he had never heard any. They didn't make conversation; rather they let a seedling of thought sprout by itself, and then watched with wonder while it sent out branching limbs. They were surprised at the strange fruit their conversation bore, for they didn't direct their thinking, nor trellis nor trim it the way so many people do.

There on the limb the three sat. Their clothes were rags and their hair was only hacked off to keep it out of their eyes. The men wore long, untrimmed beards. They watched the water-skaters on the surface of the pool below them, a pool which had been deepened by idling toes. The giant tree above them whisked softly in the wind, and occasionally dropped a leaf like a brown handkerchief. Robbie was five years old.

"I think sycamore trees are good," he observed when a leaf fell in his lap. Jakob picked up the leaf and stripped the parchment from its ribs.

"Yes," he agreed, "they grow by water. Good things love water. Bad things always been dry."

"Sycamores are big and good," said Junius. "It seems to me that a good thing or a kind thing must be very large to survive. Little good things are always destroyed by evil little things. Rarely is a big thing poisonous or treacherous. For this reason, in human thinking, bigness is an attribute of good and littleness of evil. Do you see that, Robbie?"

"Yes," said Robbie. "I see that. Like elephants."

"Elephants are often evil, but when we think of them, they seem gentle and good."

"But water," Jakob broke in. "Do you see about water too?"

"No, not about water."

"But I see," said Junius. "You mean that water is the

seed of life. Of the three elements water is the sperm, earth the womb and sunshine the mould of growth."

Thus they taught him nonsense.

The people of the Pastures of Heaven recoiled from Junius Maltby after the death of his wife and his two boys. Stories of his callousness during the epidemic grew to such proportions that eventually they fell down of their own weight and were nearly forgotten. But although his neighbours forgot that Junius had read while his children died, they could not forget the problem he was becoming. Here in the fertile valley he lived in fearful poverty. While other families built small fortunes, bought Fords and radios, put in electricity and went twice a week to the moving pictures in Monterey or Salinas, Junius degenerated and became a ragged savage. The men of the valley resented his good bottom land, all overgrown with weeds, his untrimmed fruit trees and his fallen fences. The women thought with loathing of his unclean house with its littered dooryard and dirty windows. Both men and women hated his idleness and his complete lack of pride. For a while they went to visit him, hoping by their neat examples to drag him from his slothfulness. But he received them naturally and with the friendliness of equality. He wasn't a bit ashamed of his poverty nor of his rags. Gradually his neighbours came to think of Junius as an outcast. No one drove up the private road to his house any more. They outlawed him from decent society and resolved never to receive him should he be visit them.

Junius knew nothing about the dislike of his neighbours. He was still gloriously happy. His life was as unreal, as romantic and as unimportant as his thinking. He was content to sit in the sun and to dangle his feet in the stream. If he had no good clothes, at least he had no place to go which required good clothes.

Although the people almost hated Junius, they had only pity for the little boy Robbie. The women told one another how horrible it was to let the child grow up in such squalor. But, because they were mostly good people, they felt a strong reluctance for interfering with Junius' affairs.

"Wait until he's school age," Mrs. Banks said to a group of ladies in her own parlour. "We couldn't do anything now if we wanted to. He belongs to that father of his. But just as soon as the child is six, the county'll have something to say, let me tell you."

Mrs. Allen nodded and closed her eyes earnestly. "We keep forgetting that he's Mamie Quaker's child as much as Maltby's. I think we should have stepped in long ago. But when he goes to school we'll give the poor little fellow a few things he never had."

"The least we can do is to see that he has enough clothes to cover him," another of the women agreed.

It seemed that the valley lay crouched in waiting for the time when Robbie should go to school. When, at term opening, after his sixth birthday, he did not appear, John Whiteside, the clerk of the school board, wrote a letter to Junius Maltby.

"I hadn't thought of it," Junius said when he read it. "I guess you'll have to go to school."

"I don't want to go," said Robbie.

"I know. I don't much want you to go, either. But we have laws. The law has a self-protective appendage called penalty. We have to balance the pleasure of breaking the law against the punishment. The Carthaginians punished even misfortune. If a general lost a battle through bad luck, he was executed. At present we punish people for accidents of birth and circumstance in much the same manner."

In the ensuing discussion they forgot all about the letter. John Whiteside wrote a very curt note.

"Well, Robbie, I guess you'll have to go," said Junius, when he received it. "Of course they'll teach you a great many useful things."

"Why don't you teach me?" Robbie pleaded.

"Oh, I can't. You see I've forgotten the things they teach."

"I don't want to go at all. I don't want to learn things."

"I know you don't, but I can't see any other way out."

And so one morning Robbie trudged to school. He was clad in an ancient pair of overalls, out at the knees and seat, a blue shirt from which the collar was gone, and nothing else. His long hair hung over his grey eyes like the forelock of a range pony.

The children made a circle around him in the school yard and stared at him in silence. They had all heard of the poverty of the Maltbys and of Junius' laziness. The boys looked forward to this moment when they could torture Robbie. Here was the time come; he stood in their circle, and they only stared at him. No one said, "Where'd you get them clothes," or, "Look at his hair," the way they had intended to. The children were puzzled by their failure to torment Robbie.

As for Robbie, he regarded the circle with serious eyes. He was not in the least frightened. "Don't you play games?" he asked. "My father said you'd play games."

And then the circle broke up with howls. "He doesn't know any games."—"Let's teach him pewee."—"No, nigger-baby." "Listen! Listen! Prisoner's base first."—"He doesn't know any games."

And, although they didn't know why, they thought it rather a fine thing not to know games. Robbie's thin face was studious. "We'll try pewee first," he decided. He was clumsy at the new games, but his teachers did not hoot at him. Instead they quarreled for the privilege of showing him how to hold the pewee stick. There are several schools of technique in pewee. Robbie stood aside listening for a while, and at last chose his own instructor.

Robbie's effect on the school was immediate. The older boys let him entirely alone, but the younger ones imitated him in everything, even tearing holes in the knees of their overalls. When they sat in the sun with their backs to the school wall, eating their lunches, Robbie told them about his father and about the sycamore tree. They listened intently and wished their fathers were lazy and gentle, too.

Sometimes a few of the boys, disobeying the orders of their parents, sneaked up to the Maltby place on a Saturday, Junius gravitated naturally to the sycamore limb, and, while they sat on both sides of him, he read *Treasure Island* to them, or described the Gallic wars or the battle of Trafalgar. In no time at all, Robbie, with the backing of his father, became the king of the school yard. This is demonstrated by the facts that he had no chum, that they gave him no nickname, and that he arbitrated all the disputes. So exalted was his station that no one even tried to fight with him.

Only gradually did Robbie come to realize that he was the leader of the younger boys of the school. Something self-possessed and mature about him made his companions turn to him for leadership. It wasn't long before his was the voice which decided the game to be played. In baseball he was the umpire for the reason that no other boy could make a ruling without causing a riot. And while he played the games badly himself, questions of rules and ethics were invariably referred to him.

After a lengthy discussion with Junius and Jakob, Robbie invented two vastly popular games, one called

106

Slinkey Coyote, a local version of Hare and Hounds, and the other named Broken Leg, a kind of glorified tag. For these two games he made rules as he needed them.

Miss Morgan's interest was aroused by the little boy, for he was as much a surprise in the schoolroom as he was in the yard. He could read perfectly and used a man's vocabulary, but he could not write. He was familiar with numbers, no matter how large, yet he refused to learn even the simplest arithmetic. Robbie learned to write with the greatest of difficulty. His hand wavered crazy letters on his school pad. At length Miss Morgan tried to help him.

"Take one thing and do it over and over until you get it perfectly," she suggested. "Be very careful with each letter."

Robbie searched his memory for something he liked. At length he wrote, "There is nothing so monsterous but we can belief it of ourselfs." He loved that monsterous. It gave timbre and profundity to the thing. If there were words, which through their very sound-power could drag unwilling genii from the earth, 'monsterous' was surely one of them. Over and over he wrote the sentence, putting the greatest of care and drawing on his 'monsterous.' At the end of an hour, Miss Morgan came to see how he was getting on.

"Why, Robert, where in the world did you hear that?"

"It's from Stevenson, ma'am. My father knows it by heart almost."

Of course Miss Morgan had heard all the bad stories of Junius, and in spite of them had approved of him. But now she began to have a strong desire to meet him.

Games in the school yard were beginning to fall off in interest. Robbie lamented the fact to Junius one morning before he started off to school. Junius scratched his beard and thought. "Spy is a good game," he said at last. "I remember I used to like Spy."

"Who shall we spy on, though?"

"Oh, anyone. It doesn't matter. We used to spy on Italians."

Robbie ran off excitedly to school, and that afternoon, following a lengthy recourse to the school dictionary, he organized the B.A.S.S.F.E.A.J. Translated, which it never was above a whisper, this was the Boys' Auxiliary Secret Service For Espionage Against The Japanese. If for no other reason, the very magnificence of the name of this organization would have made it a force to be reckoned with. One by one Robbie took the boys into the dim greenness under the school yard willow tree, and there swore them to secrecy with an oath so ferocious that it would have done credit to a lodge. Later, he brought the group together. Robbie explained to the boys that we would undoubtedly go to war with Japan some day.

"It behoofs us to be ready," he said. "The more we can find out about the nefarious practices of this nefarious race, the more spy information we can give our country when war breaks out."

The candidates succumbed before this glorious diction. They were appalled by the seriousness of a situation which required words like these. Since spying was now the business of the school, little Takashi Kato, who was in the third grade, didn't spend a private moment from then on. If Takashi raised two fingers in school, Robbie glanced meaningly at one of the Boy Auxiliaries, and a second hand sprung frantically into the air. When Takashi walked home after school, at least five boys crept through the brush beside the road. Eventually, however, Mr. Kato, Takashi's father, fired a shot into the dark one night, after seeing a white face looking in his window. Robbie reluctantly called the Auxiliary together and ordered that espionage be stopped at sundown. "They couldn't do anything really important at night," he explained.

In the long run Takashi did not suffer from the espionage practised on him, for, since the Auxiliaries had to watch him, they could make no important excursions without taking him along. He found himself invited everywhere, because no one would consent to be left behind to watch him.

The Boy Auxiliaries received their death blow when Takashi, who had in some way learned of their existence, applied for admittance.

"I don't see how we can let you in," Robbie explained kindly. "You see you're a Japanese, and we hate them."

Takashi was almost in tears. "I was born here, the same as you," he cried. "I'm just as good American as you, ain't I?"

Robbie thought hard. He didn't want to be cruel to Takashi. Then his brow cleared. "Say, do you speak Japanese?" he demanded.

"Sure, pretty good."

"Well, then you can be our interpreter and figure out secret messages."

Takashi beamed with pleasure. "Sure I can," he cried enthusiastically. "And if you guys want, we'll spy on my old man."

But the thing was broken. There was no one left to fight but Mr. Kato, and Mr. Kato was too nervous with his shotgun.

Hallowe'en went past, and Thanksgiving. In that time Robbie's effect on the boys was indicated by a growth in their vocabularies, and by a positive hatred for shoes or of any kind of good clothing for that matter. Although he didn't realize it, Robbie had set a style, not new, perhaps, but more rigid than it had been. It was unmanly to wear good clothes, and even more than that, it was considered an insult to Robbie.

One Friday afternoon Robbie wrote fourteen notes, and secretly passed them to fourteen boys in the school yard. The notes were all the same. They said: "A lot of indians are going to burn the Pres. of the U.S. to the stake at my house tomorrow at ten o'clock. Sneak out and bark like a fox down by our lower field. I will come and lead you to the rescue of this poor soul."

For several months Miss Morgan had intended to call upon Junius Maltby. The stories told of him, and her contact with his son, had raised her interest to a high point. Every now and then, in the schoolroom, one of the boys imparted a piece of astounding information. For example, one child who was really famous for his stupidity, told her that Hengest and Horsa invaded Britain. When pressed he admitted that the information came from Junius Maltby, and that in some way it was a kind of a secret. The old story of the goat amused the teacher so much that she wrote it for a magazine, but no magazine bought it. Over and over she had set a date to walk out to the Maltby farm.

She awakened on a December Saturday morning and found frost in the air and a brilliant sun shining. After breakfast she put on her corduroy skirt and her hiking boots, and left the house. In the yard she tried to persuade the ranch dogs to accompany her, but they only flopped their tails and went back to sleep in the sun.

The Maltby place lay about two miles away in the little canyon called Gato Amarillo. A stream ran beside the road, and sword ferns grew rankly under the alders. It was almost cold in the canyon, for the sun had not yet climbed over the mountain. Once during her walk Miss Morgan thought she heard footsteps and voices ahead of her, but when she hurried around the bend, no one was in sight. However, the brush beside the road crackled mysteriously.

Although she had never been there before, Miss Morgan knew the Maltby land when she came to it. Fences reclined tiredly on the ground under an overload of bramble. The fruit trees stretched bare branches clear of a forest of weeds. Wild blackberry vines clambered up the apple trees; squirrels and rabbits bolted from under her feet, and soft voiced doves flew away with whistling wings. In a tall wild pear tree a congress of bluejays squawked a cacophonous argument. Then, beside an elm tree which wore a shaggy coat of frost-bitten morning glory, Miss Morgan saw the mossy, curled shingles of the Maltby roof. The place, in its quietness, might have been deserted for a hundred years. "How rundown and slovenly," she thought. "How utterly lovely and slipshod!" She let herself into the yard through a wicket gate which hung to its post by one iron band. The farm buildings were grey with weathering, and, up the sides of the walls, outlawed climbers pushed their fingers. Miss Morgan turned the corner of the house and stopped in her tracks; her mouth fell open and a chill shriveled on her spine. In the center of the yard a stout post was set up, and to it an old and ragged man was bound with many lengths of rope. Another man, younger and smaller, but even more ragged, piled brush about the feet of the captive. Miss Morgan shivered and backed around the house corner again. "Such things don't happen," she insisted. "You're dreaming. Such things just can't happen." And then she heard the most amiable of conversations going on between the two men.

"It's nearly ten," said the torturer.

The captive replied, "Yes, and you be careful how you put fire to that brush. You be sure to see them coming before you light it."

111

Miss Morgan nearly screamed with relief. She walked a little unsteadily toward the stake. The free man turned and saw her. For a second he seemed surprised, but immediately recovering, he bowed. Coming from a man with torn overalls and a matted beard, the bow was ridiculous and charming.

"I'm the teacher," Miss Morgan explained breathlessly. "I was just out for a walk, and I saw this house. For a moment I thought this auto-da-fé was serious."

Junius smiled. "But it *is* serious. It's more serious than you think. For a moment I thought you were the rescue. The relief is due at ten o'clock, you know."

A savage barking of foxes broke out below the house among the willows. "That will be the relief," Junius continued. "Pardon me, Miss Morgan, isn't it? I am Junius Maltby and this gentleman on ordinary days is Jakob Stutz. Today, though, he is President of the United States being burned by Indians. For a time we thought he'd be Guenevere, but even without the full figure, he makes a better President than a Guenevere, don't you think? Besides he refused to wear a skirt."

"Damn foolishness," said the President complacently.

Miss Morgan laughed. "May I watch the rescue, Mr. Maltby?"

"I'm not Mr. Maltby, I'm three hundred Indians."

The barking of foxes broke out again. "Over by the steps," said the three hundred Indians. "You won't be taken for a redskin and massacred over there." He gazed toward the stream. A willow branch was shaking wildly. Junius scratched a match on his trousers and set fire to the brush at the foot of the stake. As the flame leaped up, the willow trees seemed to burst into pieces and each piece became a shrieking boy. The mass charged forward, armed as haphazardly and as terribly as the French people were when they stormed the Bastille. Even as the fire

112

licked toward the President, it was kicked violently aside. The rescuers unwound the ropes with fervent hands, and Jakob Stutz stood free and happy. Nor was the following ceremony less impressive than the rescue. As the boys stood at salute, the President marched down the line and to each overall bib pinned a leaden slug on which the word HERO was deeply scratched. The game was over.

"Next Saturday we hang the guilty villians who have attempted this dastardly plot," Robbie announced.

"Why not now? Let's hang 'em now!" the troop screamed.

"No, my men. There are lots of things to do. We have to make a gallows." He turned to his father. "I guess we'll have to hang both of you," he said. For a moment he looked covetously at Miss Morgan, and then reluctantly gave her up.

That afternoon was one of the most pleasant Miss Morgan had ever spent. Although she was given a seat of honour on the sycamore limb, the boys had ceased to regard her as the teacher.

"It's nicer if you take off your shoes," Robbie invited her, and it was nicer she found, when her boots were off and her feet dangled in the water.

That afternoon Junius talked of cannibal societies among the Aleutian Indians. He told how the mercenaries turned against Carthage. He described the Lacedaemonians combing their hair before they died at Thermopylae. He explained the origin of macaroni, and told of the discovery of copper as though he had been there. Finally when the dour Jakob opposed his idea of the eviction from the Garden of Eden, a mild quarrel broke out, and the boys started for home. Miss Morgan allowed them to distance her, for she wanted to think quietly about the strange gentleman.

The day when the school board visited was looked

113

forward to with terror by both the teacher and her pupils. It was a day of tense ceremony. Lessons were recited nervously and the misspelling of a word seemed a capital crime. There was no day on which the children made more blunders, nor on which the teacher's nerves were thinner worn.

The school board of the Pastures of Heaven visited on the afternoon of December 15. Immediately after lunch they filed in, looking sombre and funereal and a little ashamed. First came John Whiteside, the clerk, old and white haired, with an easy attitude toward education which was sometimes criticised in the valley. Pat Humbert came after him. Pat was elected because he wanted to be. He was a lonely man who had no initiative in meeting people, and who took every possible means to be thrown into their contact. His clothes were as uncompromising, as unhappy as the bronze suit on the seated statue of Lincoln in Washington. T. B. Allen followed, dumpily rolling up the aisle. Since he was the only merchant in the valley, his seat on the board belonged to him by right. Behind him strode Raymond Banks, big and jolly and very red of hands and face. Last in the line was Bert Munroe, the newly elected member. Since it was his first visit to the school, Bert seemed a little sheepish as he followed the other members to their seats at the front of the room.

When the board was seated magisterially, their wives came in and found seats at the back of the room, behind the children. The pupils squirmed uneasily. They felt that they were surrounded, that escape, should they need to escape, was cut off. When they twisted in their seats, they saw that the women were smiling benevolently on them. They caught sight of a large paper bundle which Mrs. Munroe held on her lap.

School opened. Miss Morgan, with a strained smile on

her face, welcomed the school board. "We will do nothing out of the ordinary, gentlemen," she said. "I think it will be more interesting to you in your official capacities, to see the school as it operates every day." Very little later, she wished she hadn't said that. Never within her recollection, had she seen such stupid children. Those who did manage to force words past their frozen palates, made the most hideous mistakes. Their spelling was abominable. Their reading sounded like the gibbering of the insane. The board tried to be dignified, but they could not help smiling a little from embarrassment for the children. A light perspiration formed on Miss Morgan's forehead. She had visions of being dismissed from her position by an outraged board. The wives in the rear smiled on, nervously, and time dripped by. When the arithmetic had been muddled and travestied, John Whiteside arose from his chair.

"Thank you, Miss Morgan," he said. "If you'll allow it, I'll just say a few words to the children, and then you can dismiss them. They ought to have some payment for having us here."

The teacher sighed with relief. "Then you do understand they weren't doing as well as usual? I'm glad you know that."

John Whiteside smiled. He had seen so many nervous young teachers on school board days. "If I thought they were doing their best, I'd close the school," he said. Then he spoke to the children for five minutes—told them they should study hard and love their teacher. It was the short and painless little speech he had used for years. The older pupils had heard it often. When it was done, he asked the teacher to dismiss the school. The pupils filed quietly out, but once in the air, their relief was too much for them. With howls and shrieks they did

115

their best to kill each other by disembowelment and decapitation.

John Whiteside shook hands with Miss Morgan. "We've never had a teacher who kept better order," he said kindly. "I think if you knew how much the children like you, you'd be embarrassed."

"But they're good children," she insisted loyally. "They're awfully good children."

"Of course," John Whiteside agreed. "By the way, how is the little Maltby boy getting along?"

"Why, he's a bright youngster, a curious child. I think he has almost a brilliant mind."

"We've been talking about him in board meeting, Miss Morgan. You know, of course, that his home life isn't all that it ought to be. I noticed him this afternoon especially. The poor child's hardly clothed."

"Well, it's a strange home." Miss Morgan felt that she had to defend Junius. "It's not the usual kind of home, but it isn't bad."

"Don't mistake me, Miss Morgan. We aren't going to interfere. We just thought we ought to give him a few things. His father's very poor, you know."

"I know," she said gently.

"Mrs. Munroe bought him a few clothes. If you'll call him in, we'll give them to him."

"Oh. No, I wouldn't—" she began.

"Why not? We only have a few little shirts and a pair of overalls and some shoes."

"But Mr. Whiteside, it might embarrass him. He's quite a proud little chap."

"Embarrass him to have decent clothes? Nonsense! I should think it would embarrass him more not to have them. But aside from that, it's too cold for him to go barefoot at this time of year. There's been frost on the ground every morning for a week."

116

"I wish you wouldn't," she said helplessly. "I really wish you wouldn't do it."

"Miss Morgan, don't you think you're making too much of this? Mrs. Munroe has been kind enough to buy the things for him. Please call him in so she can give them to him."

A moment later Robbie stood before them. His unkempt hair fell over his face, and his eyes still glittered with the fierceness of the play in the yard. The group gathered at the front of the room regarded him kindly, trying not to look too pointedly at his ragged clothes. Robbie gazed uneasily about.

"Mrs. Munroe has something to give you, Robert," Miss Morgan said.

Then Mrs. Munroe came forward and put the bundle in his arms. "What a nice little boy!"

Robbie placed the package carefully on the floor and put his hands behind him.

"Open it, Robert," T. B. Allen said sternly. "Where are your manners?"

Robbie gazed resentfully at him. "Yes, sir," he said, and untied the string. The shirts and the new overalls lay open before him, and he stared at them uncomprehendingly. Suddenly he seemed to realize what they were. His face flushed warmly. For a moment he looked about nervously like a trapped animal, and then he bolted through the door, leaving the little heap of clothing behind him. The school board heard two steps on the porch, and Robbie was gone.

Mrs. Munroe turned helplessly to the teacher. "What's wrong with him, anyway?"

"I think he was embarrassed," said Miss Morgan.

"But why should he be? We were nice to him."

The teacher tried to explain, and became a little angry

117

with them in trying. "I think, you see—why I don't think he ever knew he was poor until a moment ago."

"It was my mistake," John Whiteside apologized. "I'm sorry, Miss Morgan."

"What can we do about him?" Bert Munroe asked.

"I don't know. I really don't know."

Mrs. Munroe turned to her husband. "Bert, I think if you went out and had a talk with Mr. Maltby it might help. I don't mean you to be anything but kind. Just tell him little boys shouldn't walk around in bare feet in the frost. Maybe just a word like that'll help. Mr. Maltby could tell little Robert he must take the clothes. What do you think, Mr. Whiteside?"

"I don't like it. You'll have to vote to overrule my objection. I've done enough harm."

"I think his health is more important than his feelings," Mrs. Munroe insisted.

School closed for Christmas week on the twentieth of December. Miss Morgan planned to spend her vacation in Los Angeles. While she waited at the crossroads for a bus to Salinas, she saw a man and a little boy walking down the Pastures of Heaven road toward her. They were dressed in cheap new clothes, and both of them walked as though their feet were sore. As they neared her, Miss Morgan looked closely at the little boy, and saw that it was Robbie. His face was sullen and unhappy.

"Why, Robert," she cried. "What's the matter? Where are you going?"

The man spoke. "We're going to San Francisco, Miss Morgan."

She looked up quickly. It was Junius shorn of his beard. She hadn't realized that he was so old. Even his eyes, which had been young, looked old. But of course he was pale because the beard had protected his skin from sunburn. On his face there was a look of deep puzzlement.

"Are you going up for the Holidays?" Miss Morgan asked. "I love the stores in the city around Christmas. I could look in them for days."

"No," Junius replied slowly. "I guess we're going to be up there for good. I am an accountant, Miss Morgan. At least I was an accountant twenty years ago. I'm going to try to get a job." There was pain in his voice.

"But why do you do that?" she demanded.

"You see," he explained simply. "I didn't know I was doing an injury to the boy, here. I hadn't thought about it. I suppose I should have thought about it. You can see that he shouldn't be brought up in poverty. You can see that, can't you? I didn't know what people were saying about us."

"Why don't you stay on the ranch? It's a good ranch, isn't it?"

"But I couldn't make a living on it, Miss Morgan. I don't know anything about farming. Jakob is going to try to run the ranch, but you know, Jakob is very lazy. Later, when I can, I'll sell the ranch so Robbie can have a few things he never had."

Miss Morgan was angry, but at the same time she felt she was going to cry. "You don't believe everything silly people tell you, do you?"

He looked at her in surprise. "Of course not. But you can see for yourself that a growing boy shouldn't be brought up like a little animal, can't you?"

The bus came into sight on the highway and bore down on them. Junius pointed to Robbie. "He didn't want to come. He ran away into the hills. Jakob and I caught him last night. He's lived like a little animal too long, you see. Besides, Miss Morgan, he doesn't know how nice it will be in San Francisco."

119

The bus squealed to a stop. Junius and Robbie climbed into the back seat. Miss Morgan was about to get in beside them. Suddenly she turned and took her seat beside the driver. "Of course," she said to herself. "Of course, they want to be alone."

❦ John ❦
Steinbeck

☐	26603	**CANNERY ROW**	**$2.75**
☐	26675	**OF MICE AND MEN**	**$2.75**
☐	26444	**THE RED PONY**	**$2.50**
☐	26261	**THE PEARL**	**$2.50**

Prices and availability subject to change without notice.

Buy them at your local bookstore or use this convenient coupon for ordering:

Special Offer
Buy a Bantam Book
for only 50¢.

Now you can have Bantam's catalog filled with hundreds of titles plus take advantage of our unique and exciting bonus book offer. A special offer which gives you the opportunity to purchase a Bantam book for only 50¢. Here's how!

By ordering any five books at the regular price per order, you can also choose any other single book listed (up to a $5.95 value) for just 50¢. Some restrictions do apply, but for further details why not send for Bantam's catalog of titles today!

Just send us your name and address and we will send you a catalog!